Stacy Davidowitz

Amulet Books • New York

**For all the aspiring Color War officers,
and the Color War officers who've inspired them**

PUBLISHER'S NOTE: This is a work of fiction. Names, characters, places, and incidents are either the product of the author's imagination or are used fictitiously, and any resemblance to actual persons, living or dead, business establishments, events, or locales is entirely coincidental.

Cataloging-in-Publication Data has been applied for and may be obtained from the Library of Congress.

ISBN: 978-1-4197-2291-2

Illustrations by Melissa Manwill
Book design by Pamela Notarantonio

Inspired by the original musical *Camp Rolling Hills*

Music and lyrics by Adam Spiegel
Book and lyrics by David Spiegel & Stacy Davidowitz

Printed and bound in U.S.A.
10 9 8 7 6 5 4 3 2 1

ABRAMS The Art of Books
115 West 18th Street, New York, NY 10011
abramsbooks.com

THE CAMP ROLLING HILLS SERIES

Book One: ***Camp Rolling Hills***

Book Two: ***Crossing Over***

Book Three: ***Breakout!***

WHITE AWESOME 80s
TOTLE
General Ferrara
Jamie
Steinberg
WIENER
General Silver
Slimey
Missi

blue Psychedelic 60s
PLAY DOUGH
Gen. Power
Melman
SMELLY
Jenny
General McCarville
SOPHIE
DOVER

COLOR WAR

OFFICIAL BOOKLET

BLUE vs. WHITE

Weeklong Full-out Competition in All Things CAMP

COLOR WAR RULES

1. Campers must be supervised or with a buddy at all times.
2. Good sportsmanship.
3. No Color War in the cabin.
4. Must have permission from directors to use camp property.
5. Team rosters must be turned in for all athletics. No changes.
6. All protests must be signed by an officer.
7. Medical excuses must be decided by the camp doctor.
8. Have fun.

BREAKOUT

A surprise event at a surprise time that starts the war.

A Prayer to the Color War Gods

Reveille sounded at 7:45 A.M. Jenny popped open her eyes, climbed down from her top bunk, tickled her BFF Jamie awake, and began to dance around Faith Hill Cabin with an imaginary trumpet. Then, without anyone asking her to, she began her daily chores. According to the job chart, today she was Sweeper.

Anyone who knew Jenny was aware that this behavior was very un-Jenny-like. Normally, she'd shove earplugs in, strap an eye mask on, and ignore anyone who tried to wake her up. Earlier this summer, she was so over the obnoxious bugle sound that she threw her water bottle at the speaker. Ever since, it sounded muffled, like camp directors TJ and the Captain were drowning. But Jenny was on her very best behavior today for a very important reason: so she'd get chosen as Color War Lieutenant, aka a team leader in the annual camp-wide competition, aka the MOST HONORABLE HONOR EVER!

Color War broke out every year in a surprise way, at a surprise time. And since camp was ending in nine days, that surprise was fast approaching. Any day, any minute, any second now, the whole camp would be split into two teams, Blue versus White, and go head-to-head in sports, the Novelty Relays,

Bucket Brigade, Hatchet Hunt, Apache Relay, Rope Burn, Boating Regatta, Color Bowl, and of course, SING!

Jenny smiled to herself, remembering how Color War vocab was gibberish to people at home, like her hot boyfriend Christopher. But the thing was, once she got started telling him about a Color War memory, she couldn't stop, not even when he tried to kiss her. That's how much passion she had about it all.

"Jenny, you're so hyper this morning!" Missi yawned, stretching herself awake in downward-facing dog pose.

"Duh," Jenny said, looking around at her cabinmates. She was surprised that they were normal-morning sluggish. Sophie picked away at her eye crust. Melman slowly tied her short hair back with a green bandana. Slimey shuffled to the bathroom. Jamie had already started falling back asleep. "How are you all *not* hyper?" Jenny asked them.

And then, before they could answer, three taps over the loudspeaker bumped the Faith Hillers up a few rungs on the awake ladder. They clutched their ears.

TJ: Good morning, Rrrrrolling Hills! It's a funny, sunny day out. Fantastic weather for—

Captain: Your normal scheduled activities.

TJ: Yes, today is not special at all.

The Faith Hillers laughed all-knowingly.

Captain: We do, however, need ten more minutes to prepare breakfast. Chef Ralph had a snafu with the pancakes.

TJ: Don't worry, they will be perfectly edible.

Captain: Please take this extra time to spiff up your cabins, because after breakfast, everyone will go straight to their first Activity Period. Thank—

The PA system went off with its signature squeal. And because of the Faith Hill speaker damage, it sounded even worse—like a dying seal.

"Already sweeping!" Jenny cried, raising her broom. "Chore time, Faithers!" Her instincts were always spot-on when Color War was around the corner.

"Omigod, I really hope you're my Lieutenant," Jamie said, bending down with a dustpan. "I'm going to cry if you're not."

"Me too," Jenny said. "It's been my dream since I was in Two Tree Hill Cabin. I've never told anyone this before, but I shadowed all of my Lieutenants."

Jamie looked up with her big, wondrous eyes. "You did?"

"Yeah. Like, I watched them lead cheers, and make sports rosters, and assign campers to Apache events, and write SING songs. I recorded my observations and how I would do stuff better."

"How would you do stuff better?"

Jenny scanned the pages of her diary in her head and landed on an answer. "It's about being insanely spirited, even when you think no one's looking, because someone is always looking. At least a hundred campers will want to be me, you know?" Jenny was lowballing it because, well, she didn't want to sound too conceited.

Jamie's eyes popped open in awe. "That's a lot of pressure. I'd be so scared. Not that you should be scared. You know what I mean."

Jenny smiled. "Totally. I'm going to have to make really big decisions, and I might end up hurting people's feelings. Not yours, of course, but still. Like, not everyone was born to do the Egg Toss, you know?"

Jamie nodded. Jenny hoped she understood where she was going with this—Jamie would not be doing the Egg Toss. Sophie would, if Sophie was on her team, because even though Sophie was generally spastic, she had a lot of experience caring for egg babies in health class.

Jenny plowed on, carefully sweeping her pile into Jamie's pan. "And the thing is, I've worked really hard all summer to show that I'm an amazing leader. The Captain has no choice but to give it to me." Her mind flashed to the time she gave Melman the Princess Bethany makeover, and makeup-designed Miss(ter) Rolling Hills, and spearheaded the Sparkling Clean Initiative, turning Faith Hill Cabin dust bunny–free for Visiting Day. If this didn't qualify her for the coveted position of Lieutenant, she didn't know what did. "It's going to happen, I just know it."

"Obviously," Jamie confirmed. "The Captain would have to have memory loss or something not to give it to you."

Jenny smiled a big thanks and then bravely went to sweep toilet paper and hair from the bathroom floor. The rest of cleanup wasn't boring like normal. When the hills were buzzing with Color War anticipation, even unclogging the sink of Cup o' Noodles was fun. At least that's what Slimey had said yesterday while she was doing it.

But by the time the bugle sounded ten minutes later, letting the whole camp know that Ralph had breakfast ready, Faith Hill Cabin looked messier than when they'd started. There were six dust piles that had been scattered from reenacting last Color War's SING choreography. Sophie had reclogged the sink with the wet toilet paper she'd used to scrub the drain. And the cubbies were torn apart—the girls had fished through their clothes to separate their whites from their blues so they'd be prepared for whatever Color War team they were assigned. The pink clothes, which had been featured for six and a half weeks, were temporarily shoved to the back. Melman, being the anti-pink tomboy she was, seemed thrilled about this.

"So when do you think Color War's going to break?" she asked the group as they walked to breakfast. "Let's take bets."

"Lunchtime," Slimey said, sticking a leaf into her bedhead ponytail. "We're going to walk into the Dining Hall, and there's going to be blue and white disco lights! The themes are going to be *Saturday Night Fever* versus . . . uh . . . Real Fever!"

Jenny doubted that. Considering how sunny it would be at noon and how many windows the Dining Hall had, disco lights would barely show. Plus, last summer, Color War broke in the Dining Hall. TJ and the Captain rode in on donkeys. The teams and themes and officers were announced in packets taped under the tables. Another Dining Hall Breakout would be lame. "No," Jenny said.

"I think it'll happen tonight!" Missi squealed, halting halfway up a mini-hill to look at Jenny for approval. Jenny gave her no such thing. Her first summer, Breakout had happened during an Evening Activity hosted by Mercutio Solomon, the touring summer camp magician, and that had only worked because the whole camp was in the Social Hall to watch him empty the Color War packets from his supposedly empty hat. Tonight, every age group had a different Evening Activity scattered about camp.

Missi carried on, unfazed. "If you look at the calendar in the HC, under tonight's Evening Activity for the Faith and Hamburger Hillers, the Captain wrote 'TBD,' which she said stands for 'The Beading Demolition,' but, like, the Arts and Crafts shack has been sealed off. They're obviously using it to make the Color War banners."

"What's 'The Beading Demolition'?" Jamie asked, totally naive like always.

Missi scrunched her nose in thought. "Um."

"There's no such thing as 'The Beading Demolition,'" Jenny snapped, wondering if she really was the only one who understood how camp worked. "The Captain was messing with you."

Missi smiled, embarrassed. Then she laughed, a little delayed.

"'The Bot Day,'" Sophie offered, which was no surprise. All summer she'd been obsessed with her award-winning robot, Georgina. "You can never have too many robo-activities!"

Everyone ignored her.

"It could also mean 'The Big Day,'" Slimey suggested, just as clueless.

"Yeah, but the Captain's smarter than that," Melman said. "'TBD' has gotta be more cryptic."

"'TBD' means 'To Be Decided,'" Jenny said flatly. "Do you all seriously not know that?" She took in a breath of fresh mountain air and moved on. "Who do you think the Lieutenants will be?" While she waited for them to answer, she sang in her head, *Me, me, me, me, me.* She saw Lieutenant as part of her hard-earned destiny. At home, before she'd turned double digits, she'd shed all the uncool things about her. Only then was she able to befriend Willamena, the Most Popular girl in all of Roslyn. And now, here at camp, Jenny was Most Popular. Girls like her were meant to use their popularity for good in positions such as: Head Cheerleader, Homecoming Queen, Miss Long Island, Miss America, Miss World, and Miss Universe. She'd studied the system. Being Lieutenant just made sense.

Slimey shrugged. "I think it could be any of us. I mean, we're all pretty great."

"Aw, Slimes," Melman said. She crouched down, and Slimey hopped onto her back. "*You're* great."

Jenny rolled her eyes.

Missi and Jamie spoke in unison: "I think Jenny!" Then, in unison: "Jinx!" And then, because that was in unison: "Double jinx!" Then they broke into laughter, ran ahead, and forgot all about Jenny. She felt a pinch of jealousy. And then felt dumb for being jealous of Missi of all people, as if she were a threat to the unbreakable J-squad.

The only one who hadn't answered was weirdo Sophie. Jenny hung back while Sophie and their Scottish counselor, Scottie, finished a game of thumb war. Sophie had dipped her entire left thumb in white nail polish and her entire right thumb in blue nail polish and was apparently competing with both thumbs to predict who would win Color War. Because Sophie was ambidextrous, aka both-handed, neither thumb had the advantage. Neither color won. Scottie beat her both times. Then they continued to trudge uphill.

"Hey, Sophster," Jenny purred, sidling up between them. "Who do you think is going to be Lieutenant?"

"Scottie."

"Thank you, my lady," Scottie said in her wacky accent, which was the normal way she spoke.

"Scottie can't be Lieutenant," Jenny told Sophie impatiently. As a fifth-year camper, Sophie should know this. Jenny explained to Scottie, "Counselors are only up for Generals, and they don't give first-year counselors General. It's something you earn after being here for a lot of years."

"Then me," Sophie said.

"Then you what?" Jenny asked.

"Then I'll be Lieutenant," Sophie said.

Jenny laughed and then tried to cover it up as a cough. If Sophie were Lieutenant, it would be loser chaos. Everyone would wear robot costumes and vampire fangs, regardless of the theme. "Cool. That's amazing you have so much self-confidence."

Sophie nodded.

"But, OK, who else? There's going to be one Blue and one White Lieutenant in Faith Hill."

Sophie gazed at their cabinmates, now a full mini-hill away. "I think Slimey."

Jenny narrowed her eyes. She feared Slimey might get picked over her, because Slimey was like a commercial for positivity and friendship. But Jenny had been trying not to think about that, because stress gave her chin pimples. The last time she got a chin pimple, she'd begged her mom to let her go on Accutane like Willamena's older sister, but her mom had told her she was even more perfect with all of her imperfections. It was a totally delusional thing to say. Delusion didn't get a Popular girl anywhere. It was time to face the truth. "Why?"

"Let's see . . . ," Sophie started. Jenny crossed her fingers that Sophie would say something irrelevant like "Because Slimey is a bloodsucking robot and that's neato." But instead she said, "Because she's nice and friends with everyone and a good artist."

"That's true," Scottie confirmed, as if Jenny hadn't known Slimey for four summers and this was news.

"Or Melman," Sophie added.

"Or Melman what?" Jenny asked.

"Or Melman could be Lieutenant."

Jenny wished she'd never hung back to ask Sophie. Yes, Melman was the sportiest, most intense Faith Hiller. Obviously. Jenny didn't need it rubbed in her face. But oblivious to Jenny's chin pimple in the making, Sophie blabbed on: "Melman has calves of steel and the short hair of a brave soldier. Who wouldn't pick her?"

It took a second, but then Jenny sighed with relief. Everyone knew you didn't need exceptional leg muscles or a boy haircut to be Lieutenant. There was a reason TJ and the Captain chose one boy and one girl from every cabin for each team. It was called *balance*. Also, hadn't Melman gotten enough attention this summer with Ghost Court, and making out with Totle, and pretending to be Melvin the Soccer Stud? Surely the camp directors would want to spread the love. "Well, if we're both Lieutenants," Jenny told Sophie, "you'd better watch your back."

Sophie patted her own back, and then pointed at Jenny with an enormous smile. "You watch your front!" Then she waited for Jenny to pat her front or something, which Jenny was not about to do.

Jenny, Sophie, and Scottie walked up and down one last hill before they reached the Dining Hall. By the time they joined the rest of the Faith Hillers at their table, Jenny felt a little deflated. She munched on some Froot Loops while she waited for the hot trays to be served, hoping that might lift her spirits, but the cereal just tasted like crunchy medicine. Ugh. Jenny wanted everyone to believe in her, not just Jamie and Missi, who had to believe in her because they were her Best Friend and Wannabe Best Friend. She guessed she'd have to prove her amazingness during the war.

Jenny was suddenly distracted by a commotion at a table up front and accidentally swallowed three Froot Loops whole. She darted her eyes to another commotion at a table in the back. Then at some tables in the middle. The Dining Hall erupted into gasps and screams. Everyone seemed to be hovering over their breakfast trays. What was up with the pancakes? Had Ralph had another snafu? As Scottie lowered the tray to the table, Jenny snatched off the metal lid, revealing . . . blue and white pancakes! She lit up like a Hanukkah bush. This was not a drill! Color War was about to break!

The Dining Hall erupted: *"ONE, TWO, THREE, FOUR! WE WANT COLOR WAR!"*

Jenny stood on top of the table, stomping and clapping and screaming the loudest of all the Faith Hillers, maybe even the whole camp. But then it occurred to her that, as Lieutenant, she would need the full range of her voice. She took it down a notch volume-wise, but exaggerated her lips so that she still looked spirit-crazy. *"Five, six, seven, eight! We don't want to wait!"*

Jamie jumped up to Jenny's side so fast she made a fork fly off the table. "I'm so excited, but I'm also worried we're going to be separated," Jamie said. "Like, you won't be *my* Lieutenant."

Jenny pulled Jamie in for a hug. She smelled like the organic gummy bear vitamins her mom made her take every morning so she'd grow boobs like other thirteen-year-olds. "If they separate us, it's only because together we're too powerful."

Jamie pinched her skinny arm where a bicep was supposed to be. "Are you sure?"

"I'm as sure as you are pretty," Jenny said. "Still, I'll freak out if you're not on my team. Can you imagine me leading without you? Who would be my second-in-command?"

Jamie shrugged with a smile, and together they scanned the Dining Hall. Jenny beamed, taking in her future subjects, all of them infected with the prewar spirit bug. Missi was clapping two spoons together. Slimey was doing the Twist. Sophie was balancing a pancake on her face. Scottie was whipping her bandana in the air. Melman was juggling her muddy soccer ball (spirited, but unsanitary). Literally, everyone was on a table or bench, chanting: *"One, two, three, four! We want Color War!"* Jenny would never tell Jamie this, but she knew in her heart of hearts that any Faith Hiller could be her second-in-command. A good enough leader could help anyone, even a follower like Missi, step into her leadership role.

Though, in a perfect camp world, Missi would be on the opposite team of her and Jamie. Jenny was tired of watching the two of them bond over being tone-deaf, and loving kitties on YouTube, and campaigning for Jenny's Lieutenantship. It was time that Missi got a reminder of her place as awkward third wheel. BFF stood for Best Friend Forever, and like in Color War, there was only ever one Best, and that was always Jenny.

Two taps over the PA system made everyone's heads snap to the middle of the Dining Hall. There stood TJ and the Captain in front of a mountain of single-serving cereal containers. TJ was wearing head-to-toe white and the Captain was wearing head-to-toe blue. Not just camp-colored clothes, but also face paint, body paint, wigs, pom-poms—the whole shebang. Rolling Hills nearly lost their minds, Jenny included. She'd momentarily forgotten about saving her voice—she had the prewar bug, too, and there was just no stomping it out!

From the Boys' Side of the Dining Hall, Jenny could hear the Hamburger Hillers chanting: *"Play Dough for Lieutenant! Ooh! Ah!"* She stood on her tippy toes to catch a glimpse of

Play Dough doing the cha-cha dance on top of his table. He seemed so *confident.* Was it because his friends believed in him? Because they supported him with all their hearts and cheers? Why couldn't Jenny's cabinmates do the same for her? She squeezed Jamie's hand to give her a hint. But Jamie just squeezed back. Jenny tried to be more obvious. "Look at Play Dough!" She laughed. "The Hamburger boys are all cheering for him!"

"I can't see!" Jamie whined, jumping as high as she could, which was still shorter than Jenny when Jenny had her feet planted.

So Jenny started the chant for herself, making intense eye contact with all of her cabinmates so they'd join in. They all did. First Missi and Jamie, then Sophie and Slimey, and then Melman. *"Jenny for Lieutenant! Ooh! Ah!"* And it felt amazing! Jenny threw her arms up, and her head, too, and right in her line of sight, on the wall were the Color War plaques dating all the way back to 1965. The Lieutenants listed on them were probably grandparents now! Jenny thought about how one day when she was a grandma, she'd send her grandkids to Rolling Hills, and they'd spot JENNY NOLAN on this summer's plaque and dream of making it up there themselves. And then *their* grandkids would come to Rolling Hills and dream of it, too. War was cyclical, she'd learned in social studies, and she finally understood what that meant.

But suddenly Jenny stopped hearing her name, and all the amazingness she'd felt vanished. Melman switched the chant to promote Slimey, and Slimey switched the chant to promote

Melman, and then, little by little, the whole Dining Hall was chanting for different Lieutenants, like it was a job that could literally be anyone's and wasn't reserved for the best, most special Upper Campers.

Before Jenny had a chance to protest, TJ broke through the mash of Lieutenant-requesting cheers with a "Can I get a *Moooooo*?"

Yes, Jenny knew *moooooo*-ing made zero sense. But weird randomness was a general rule of thumb at camp, especially when Color War was on the brink of breaking. So it was no surprise that everyone, herself included, responded on cue: *"MOOOOOOO!"*

The Captain was using every muscle in her face to keep from laughing.

"Can I get a *Bahhhhhhh*?" TJ asked.

"BAHHHHHHH!"

The Captain buried her face in her hands, convulsing.

TJ began to rap, crowning the Captain with a Froot Loops container he'd found at his feet. *"My wife, my love, my dairy queen! This Color War is milk-themed!"*

Milk-themed? Last summer, the themes were White Land of Oz versus Blue Far Far Away. And the summer before that: White Apps versus Blue Board Games. What could TJ mean? Like White Cow Milk versus Blue Goat Milk? It seemed kind of limiting. Especially considering how many campers were lactose intolerant.

TJ's voice boomed into the mic: "White Creamer versus Blue Yogurt!" The camp mumbled in confusion. There was some laughter, some screaming cheers. "The Generals and the Lieutenants are listed—"

Listed where?! Jenny hyperventilated.

"—inside the milk cartons on your table!"

Jenny darted her eyes to the 2% milk by Slimey's feet. Slimey's fingers were already going toward it, so Jenny had to act fast. She threw herself across the table, smushing the pancakes under her belly, and grabbed hold of the milk first. She sat up so that the carton would be out of Slimey's reach, and with no time to waste, flipped it over to get a look at the inside.

The milk poured all over her face. Jenny didn't even care. In fact, as the milk cascaded down her chin and onto her shirt, she thought about how, if she were a White Lieutenant, everyone would praise her for her commitment to the team! If she were on Blue, well, she'd have to duck into the shower. Or get her hands on some blueberry yogurt. When the last of the milk smacked off her eyes, a laminated card fell out of the carton. In black Sharpie it read: FAKEOUT.

No, Jenny thought. *No, no, no, no, NO!*

The entire camp broke into: *"FAKEOUT, FAKEOUT, WE WANT A BREAKOUT!"* They chanted it over and over.

Jenny looked up at her cabinmates, who were keeling over with laughter. At her. She was covered in milk and blue pancakes. For nothing. The break was fake, and the war had not begun.

"Aw, Jenny!" Melman said, giving her a hand that Jenny pretended not to see. "That was obviously a Fakeout. Milk-themed Color War? Really? We all saw the Captain. She could barely contain herself, the whole thing was so far-fetched."

Missi wrung out an especially soaked clump of Jenny's hair. "Well, as someone who milks cows and goats, I believed TJ and thought the dairy theme was super-trendy."

Jenny wanted to whip her milky hair across Missi's face.

"I had no idea it was a Fakeout," Jamie said, sitting beside Jenny but far enough away so that she didn't get milk on her. She was one of the Intolerants.

"Yeah, well, I knew it was a Fakeout," Jenny lied, hopping down off the table. "I'm not stupid. I was just getting in the spirit to, like, be a good role model for Lower Camp."

She watched Slimey and Melman exchange one of their looks they assumed no one ever noticed, and then Jenny looked at Jamie for support. But Jamie was chewing the inside of her cheek, and beside her, Missi was looking down at her feet. Jenny felt a pinch of guilt. She hadn't meant to call them stupid. Well, not Jamie at least. "Jamie and Missi knew it was a Fakeout, too. They were just defending me because they're amazing friends, especially Jamie."

Jamie and Missi looked up, all smiles.

Friendship comes so naturally to me, Jenny thought. *I really will make the best Lieutenant.*

When the Faith Hillers headed to their first Activity Period, lacrosse, Jenny walked toward the cabin to shower. Before she climbed the porch steps, she clasped her fingers together, looked up at a cloud shaped like a meerkat, and prayed: "Hi, Color War Gods. It's me, Jenny. So, I'm assuming you guys are going to break this war, like, now, so I just want to remind you that I deserve to be Lieutenant and would be the best at it. Thank you so much for listening. Amen." And then the meerkat cloud morphed into a *J* cloud, and Jenny hugged herself, assured that everything she'd ever wanted was going to be hers.

When It's in Your Blood

"Tonight's Evening Activity is called 'The Bandit's Deal'!" Yoshi announced to the Faith Hill and Hamburger Hill campers gathered on the basketball court bleachers.

Play Dough heard an eruption of girly giggles from the Faith Hillers, and he had no idea why. He guessed they were making fun of Counselor Yoshi's enthusiasm for a dumb activity no one wanted to play.

"So this isn't just a cover for Color War break?" Melman asked Yoshi, who looked back at her with an *I can't tell you* smile. Play Dough found that extremely annoying, because there was no way in smellzone that first-year counselor Yoshi knew his blues from his whites, let alone when the war was going to get started. That secret was safely locked in TJ's and the Captain's minds. If Yoshi thought he knew something they all didn't, he was suffering from brain jam.

"So, the game," Yoshi began. "Boys and girls line up on opposite sides of the court. Each boy and girl is assigned a number, one through six. When I call your number, you run to the middle of the court and try to steal this." He motioned to Scottie, who tossed him a basketball. "Once you've got the ball safely to your side, your team gets a point. Got it?"

"This is just Steal the Bacon," Dover said matter-of-factly.

"Without the bacon," Play Dough said.

"Will there be bacon?" Totle asked Yoshi.

"No," Yoshi said.

"Kosher bacon?" Wiener asked.

"No," Yoshi said.

That's when the guys began to boo and the girls began to twist each other's hair and make their hands into tunnels for secrets.

It was time to take control of this programming hiccup. "This Evening Activity blows!" Play Dough announced. He hopped down from the bleachers to poll his friends. "Raise your hand if you want to play Steal the Bacon with no bacon." No hands. "Raise your hand if you want to play Knockout." All the hands.

Yoshi looked at Scottie in a panic. She just shrugged and went to get a second basketball for the game. "OK, good idea, Play Dough," Yoshi said, pretending he had control over the matter. "Play Dough with the great ideas! The Bandit's Deal is fun for another time."

Play Dough didn't want his counselor to feel totally overthrown, so he threw him a high five. Fortunately, Yoshi smiled and tossed Play Dough the basketball and no one's feelings were broken.

So everyone began to play Knockout, a shooting hoops elimination game, every man for himself. And Play Dough was having an awesome time. Unlike Color War, where every game was worth valuable team points, in Knockout, if you lost, you got to sit out and flirt with unathletic, hot girls like Jenny, his Crush Since Bunker Hill.

Which is what happened in the third game, when Jenny got out by Melman, and then Play Dough got out by Totle and met Jenny on the third row of the bleachers. He noticed her hair looked very straight today, like she'd used her illegal flat iron. He felt it. It was the yellow of Fritos, but smooth like spaghetti.

"Um, what are you doing?" Jenny asked, tossing his hand from her hair.

"Flirting," he admitted.

To his surprise, Jenny laughed. At first, that made Play Dough feel like a million bucks. But then he got paranoid that Jenny was laughing at him in a *You're such a dumb fatty* kind of way, like skinny punks in Great Neck did.

"Omigod, putting your fingers in my hair without my permission is not flirting," Jenny said, still laughing.

Play Dough noted this. Next time, he'd ask Jenny before he felt her pasta-soft hair. "Cool."

"Are you excited to be Lieutenant?" she asked him.

He gaped at her. How did she know he was going to be Lieutenant? Did she have access to TJ's and the Captain's brains? He guessed if anyone could get a peek in, it would be her. Jenny was too pretty to say no to.

"Play Dough, hello?"

"Oh. Yeah. Hello. I mean, yes. I dunno." Play Dough thought

about sticking his head in a toilet and giving himself a swirly. At camp he was normally a smooth talker, but when it came to Jenny, his words always seemed to get jammed up, like when he ate mozzarella sticks too fast. "How do you know I'm going to be Lieutenant?" he finally managed to ask.

Jenny smacked her hands to her lap. "Um, because you're Play Dough."

Play Dough cocked his head, confused. He got why his friends thought he'd be Lieutenant. He was loud and bossy and good at making fast decisions, like, for instance, switching out the Bandit's Deal for Knockout. And he got why his family thought he'd be Lieutenant. He had a long genetic history of Color War officers: Gramps Garfink in 1965, Great-Uncle Garfink in 1968, Aunt Denise in 1984, and Pops in 1985. All of them had been on White. All of them had won.

Throughout the summer, he'd gotten packages with lucky Color War paraphernalia from each of their reigns: postcards, photographs, and even Gramps Garfink's White Broadway SING packet with the lyrics of the march (an upbeat, rallying song) and the alma mater (a slow, sentimental ballad). Before leaving for camp, Play Dough got so pumped, he'd asked to try on his Gramps' Color War shirt with GENERAL GARFINK ironed onto the back, but he'd been denied access. Either Gramps didn't want his grandson to stretch it out, or it really was in vacuum-sealed-plastic protection.

But now, Play Dough was starting to get nervous about it all. No Garfinks had been officers in the twenty-first century, and his whole family was banking on him to carry on the legacy:

(1) He had to be Lieutenant. (2) He had to be on White. (3) He had to win. So naturally, every time someone told him he had Lieutenant in the bag, or speculated teams, or mentioned Blue's three-summer winning streak, his armpits threw their own private pool party. Especially when that probing someone was Jenny. *Jenny!* He had to respond to her *Um, because you're Play Dough*, and stop thinking about his wet pits. "Yeah, I'm Play Dough," he confirmed.

Jenny just looked at him, and Play Dough just looked at her. Seconds went by. Suddenly, Jenny burst out laughing again, like Play Dough had made some legendary joke, and Play Dough felt like another million bucks. That was, until he remembered that Jenny had a dumb boyfriend named Christopher, whom she'd met on a Disney cruise right before last summer. It occurred to Play Dough that Christopher probably looked like a prince and not the Pillsbury Doughboy, and so all of this Apparently Awesome Flirting was a waste of time.

Play Dough stood up, thinking he'd join Steinberg, who was developing an algorithm to determine when Color War would break.

But before he had a chance to hop off the bleachers, Jenny TOUCHED HIS ARM and said, "What about me?"

"Yeah, yup," Play Dough answered, having no clue what Jenny was asking. His brain was melting, maybe.

"So you think I'll be Lieutenant, too?" she asked, grinning expectantly.

Oh. Negative. Slimey probably, maybe Melman. Missi, even. But not Jenny. She sat out or got out in most sports because of injured braces and laziness, and was kind of intimidating to be around. But he didn't want to make her grin disappear or mess up his time in the spotlight, so he nodded. "Definitely."

Jenny's face exploded into an even bigger grin. "Omigod, what if we're Lieutenants together?!"

Play Dough could hardly believe it. Jenny wanted to be co-Lieutenants! That was a big deal. Right? He looked around, hoping Totle or Smelly was nearby and had heard her, too, but they were still in the game. "Then it will be the greatest Color War ever," he said with a salute. And he meant it.

Suddenly self-conscious that he was standing and she was sitting, Play Dough sat back down. But then Jamie pranced over and he stood back up. Jamie had always weirded him out—she reminded him of a gerbil with human sunglasses. Little people should not wear big-people clothes.

"What took you so long?" Jenny asked Jamie. "I was just sitting here alone, and I missed your munchkin face."

Alone? Jenny was by herself for only a minute before he'd joined her. He stayed quiet about it, which made him feel invisible, and not in a superhero way.

"I won!" Jamie cried with little-gerbil joy.

"You won what?" Jenny asked.

"Knockout!!!"

Jenny chuckled in disbelief, and in attempt to feel visible again, Play Dough chuckled, too.

"No way!" Jenny squealed to Jamie. "Honestly, Dover probably let you win because he has a crush on you."

Play Dough noted two things. First, Jamie was so pissed,

her face morphed into that of a troll's. Second, Dover did not have a crush on Jamie. He had a crush on no one.

Jamie wandered off to Missi, who was tucked under Wiener's arm and giggling like a hyena. Then she did that tunnel-for-secrets thing through Missi's frizzy red hair where Missi's ear was hiding.

Meanwhile, Jenny was watching them, seemingly contemplating the world's most evil prank. *Sour-sauce*, Play Dough thought. *My Jenny Fantasy Flirtball has reached Game Over*. But then, by some miracle, she turned to him with a smile, like she didn't have a care in the camp world. "What team do you think we'll be Lieutenants for?" she asked sweetly.

"I hope White," Play Dough replied. He was about to explain his family history and the fact that they'd always led the White team to victory, but Jenny broke in.

"Yeah, I look really good in white." She lifted her sweatshirt, and underneath, Play Dough could see she was sporting a white T-shirt. "But I also look good in blue." She peeled down her sweatpants, revealing blue leggings. The whole clothes-lifting/-peeling thing was making Play Dough nuts. "I'm so prepared for this war!"

Play Dough sunk his sweaty back into the bleachers. "Me too," he confided, emptying his shorts pockets. Stuffed in one was a white face-paint stick and in the other was a white bandana. "We're both a little crazy, huh?"

Jenny raised her eyebrows mischievously. "It's Color War," she said. "Crazy is the only way."

August 11th

Dear Christopher,

How r u? Camp is cray right now because Color War is about to break, and I'm about to be Lieutenant. When I'm Lieutenant, can u send me flowers? Thnx. If u can add a message, just write "I heart Jenny Loo-Loo" or something cute. Get it? "Loo-Loo" is short for "Lieutenant." Hahaha. Roses r best.

Actually, go online to the Rolling Hills website, and check which color I'm Lieutenant for. If I'm on White, send me white roses. If I'm on Blue, send me blue roses.

Also, happy sweet SIXTEEN months! Here's a drawing Slimey made of us. We're both waaaayy hotter in real life, but, whatevs. She's not a professional yet. Oh, also I told everyone u have tattoos!!!!!

Ur my bae,

Jenny

On the Brink

Jenny had almost pulled her flat-ironed bangs out waiting for her cabin to fall asleep.

Sophie had conked out first, sleep-mumbling about Shakespeare's allergies. Slimey and Melman had been under Melman's sheets-turned-fort, chortling about art or soccer or whatever. Then, probably because art and soccer are not chortle-worthy, they'd split ways and gone to bed. Missi had drifted off sometime before Jamie stole her leftover Visiting Day candy. Now Missi slept with two gummy kittens buried in her frizz, thanks to Jenny's dare and Jamie's obedience. And Jamie was latched on to Missi's waist, cuddle-spoon style, fast asleep.

Jenny thought it was strange that Jamie had chosen to snuggle with Missi tonight. She told herself that it wasn't personal—Jamie probably wanted to give Missi some extra love to make up for the gummy bear prank. But whatever the reason, this could not, would not, bccome habit.

Scottie released three thunderous snores, and no one budged or threw socks at her face to quiet her. Finally, Jenny was safe! She whipped out her diary from inside her pillowcase, switched her book lamp on, and reviewed her most recent entry.

Jenny's Breakout Predictions

~~August 8th – At BBQ dinner~~

~~August 9th – At reveille~~

~~August 10th – During afternoon snack~~

~~August 11th – At breakfast~~

August 11th – At Evening Activity (TBD)

She crossed out the last prediction and added:

August 12th — ANYTIME — I DON'T KNOW!!!

With camp coming to a close, every second that passed was cutting into serious Color War time. When the when was it going to break?! Jenny flipped backward to her "Faith Hillers—Strengths and Weaknesses" page. She'd folded the page over, which everyone knew was code for "TOP SECRET: GET OUT OF MY HEAD." (Just in case, she'd also written it on the flap.) She hadn't told Jamie, but she'd observed all of her cabinmates during last summer's Color War and this summer's activities, and had ranked them—1 being sucky, 5 being amazing. It wasn't personal. It was for war.

	Jenny	Jamie	Missi	Sophie	Melman	Slimey
Singing (SING)	5	2	1	4	2	3
Dancing (SING)	5	4	1	2	2	3.5
Art Stuff (SING Scenery & Costumes)	5	3	3	2	1	5
BOATING (Regatta)	5	1	3	4	5	3.5
Knowing Random Facts (Color Bowl-Trivia)	5	0	3	4	4	3
Sports (Athletic Stuff, Apache)	5	0	4	2	5	3
Finding Stuff (Hatchet Hunt)	5	2	3	4	4	3
Spirit	5	4	4	3	4	4
Sportsmanship	5	4	4	4	4	4
Leadership	5	0	1	1	4	4
TOTAL SCORES	50/50	20/50	27/50	30/50	35/50	36/50

You can't argue with numbers, Jenny thought, gazing at her perfect score. *I've reinvented myself to be a shining star.* She thought about how Lieutenant Nolan and her arm candy,

Christopher, would make the best celebrity couple. Then Jenny's night-dream was interrupted by a flashlight beaming in her face from the bed next to her.

"Omigosh, Jenny, are you up, too?" Missi asked.

Jenny was clearly up, shielding her face from blindness with her diary. "Can you stop with the flashlight, please? I'm going to have an eye seizure."

"That sounds dangerous, sorry," Missi said, lowering the flashlight to her comforter. It cast a creepy shadow across the cabin that kind of looked like witch fingers.

Jenny didn't feel like pointing that out. She didn't want to deal with Missi bringing it up tomorrow, like it was some amazing inside joke they'd shared because they were both insomniacs or whatever. "I'm going to sleep now," Jenny said. "We've got a big day tomorrow. Probably."

"Definitely probably!" Missi squealed. "The biggest day since the very first day of camp all those summers ago. Everything's been building to this Color War. We're finally old enough to be Lieutenants! Do you remember when Jamie and I first became friends with you?" Jenny did remember, but Missi rambled on before Jenny could even nod. "You knew nothing about camp. The word 'Breakout' might as well have been Portuguese! Good times. Oh, man, I'm so hyper right now, it's hard to get my brain to chillax."

"Well, try."

"Ugh. I guess I'll just count a bazillion more sheep. Once, I actually did count a bazillion sheep. It took six hours and twenty—"

"OK, night!" Jenny said. She turned off her book lamp, collapsed her diary, shoved it into her pillowcase, and closed her eyes. Then she listened to Missi whisper-count sheep up to ninety-two, at which point Missi erupted into whistles through the gap in her front teeth.

Amid the orchestra of breathing, snoring, and whistling, Jenny fell into her very first memories of Camp Rolling Hills, four summers ago, on the bus ride up to camp. Jamie had been sitting all alone, her eyes bleary from saying good-bye to her parents in the Roosevelt Field mall parking lot. Jenny, who'd been sort of relieved to part from Willamena for eight weeks, but nervous about keeping up the cool facade in order to make new friends, had sat beside Jamie and told her that she cried like a Disney princess—dramatic, but still really pretty. That made Jamie laugh, and then she didn't cry again the rest of the ride.

Within days, they had become so attached at the hip that they'd sometimes climb inside Sophie's oversize *Annie* T-shirt and tell the rest of Two Tree Hill Cabin that they were Siamese twins separated at birth. Sophie would then launch into why that was medically impossible, while the two of them giggled until their stomachs ached. Their counselor always got them confused—would call each by the other's name—until they suggested she call both of them "J." One late night the "J"s were in the bathroom testing lipstick colors on toilet paper and Missi complained: "The J-squad is keeping me awake!" And the name stuck! *Ah, memories!*

Jenny fast-forwarded to that first summer's Color War, and

the next summer's, and the next, letting all of her sizzling anticipation about tomorrow simmer into a deep, colorful, Color War Eve sleep.

In what felt like zero minutes later, she shot up to screaming sirens. Her heart was racing. Her breath was stale. Her mind was moving in slow motion.

"What time is it?" Jamie mumbled, holding Missi's mooshi pillow over her ears.

Jenny went to check her alarm clock, but then remembered that she didn't have an alarm clock at camp. She only had a backup celly, which was dead inside a shoe box under her bed. "Um, um." She could see the tiniest bit of twilight peek through the window by the front door, so it was definitely not the middle of the night, but nowhere near normal 7:45 reveille wake-up, either. "Like, really early," Jenny told Jamie.

"Omigod, WHIIIIHHHYYYYY?"

And that's when the morning fog defogged from Jenny's head. Could it have been that there was an emergency? An explosion? Dead people? Maybe. But the timing was too coincidental. There was only one real reason sirens would be sounding: COLOR WAR BREAKOUT!!!!!!!!!!!!

Jenny screamed louder than the sirens and ran out of Faith Hill Cabin in her pink onesie. She didn't know where she was running to. But then Melman quickly caught up and passed her, heading in the direction of Forest Hill, which overlooked the lake. Jenny wasn't interested in following anyone, let alone Melman. But at least if Melman was wrong and they missed everything because Breakout was actually at the Social Hall or something, no one would blame Jenny for misleading them.

"Jenny, wait!" she heard Jamie cry from far, far away. Stopping short, Jenny glanced over her shoulder. Slimey and Missi were holding hands and running behind Jenny. Behind them was Scottie. Behind her was Sophie. And then, all the way in the back, tripping on her ratty pajama pants and drowning in Jenny's sweatshirt, was Jamie.

Jenny thought about running back to Jamie so they could experience Breakout together, but then what kind of first impression would she be making as Lieutenant? She was expected to *lead*, not *wait forever* for her uncoordinated bestie. Color War wasn't the time to be charitable to one person. It was the time to be a spirit-crazy role model for the whole camp. So Jenny kept running, faster and faster, until she was so out of breath that she made a mental list of everyone she knew with an inhaler (just Steinberg) in case she arrived a wheezing, asthmatic mess.

As Jenny approached the valley of Forest Hill, a blur of bodies stampeded toward her from all cabin directions. The wailing sirens were coming from the other side of the hill. She could see Melman halfway up the hill already, and behind her, she caught a glimpse of Missi's red frizz and Sophie's octopus head of braids, but it was hard to spot anyone else. Especially someone as short as Jamie.

For a moment, Jenny worried that Jamie had gotten trampled. But then she assured herself that Jamie was so slow, she was probably all the way in the back with the One Tree Hillers. If no one was behind her, then there'd be no way she could get trampled! Jenny sighed with relief and kept shoving upward through the masses.

Just when she thought her legs might give out, she reached the peak of Forest Hill. And it was . . . *wow.* The insanely pretty view was the only thing keeping her jello legs from collapsing. The sunrise peeked up from behind Harold Hill and cast pink streaks across the sky. It reflected onto the lake like a mirror. The air smelled like dew and dandelions. It would have been the most peaceful experience ever if not for the stampede of screaming people. And the sirens. But Jenny didn't actually wish for peace at this moment. She wished for war. So it was all perfect just the way it was.

And then, as if the Color War Gods had heard Jenny's thoughts, there was a *thump-thump-thump* in the air. Jenny gazed up as a helicopter flew over Anita Hill . . . Faith Hill . . . Harold Hill, and then hovered right above Forest Hill. Her mouth hung open in disbelief. Her bangs thrashed around her forehead from the whipping blades. Her eyes teared up with anticipation and joy and sensitivity to gusts of dirty wind.

Just when Jenny thought the Breakout couldn't get any more surreal, buckets of blue and white ping-pong balls were dumped from the helicopter. She threw her arms in the air and opened and closed her fingers like crab claws, hoping to catch them raining from the sky. In the winter, she'd play

Hanukkah ping-pong with all of her cousins. No! She'd display the balls beside her dance trophies. No! She'd store them in her camp memorabilia box for her future grandkids!

But Jenny quickly forgot about the balls when hundreds of scrolls wrapped in blue ribbons began dropping instead. One smacked her right between the eyes and fell to the ground. She clawed at the other clawing fingers around her, grabbed a scroll and clutched it tight. She slid off the ribbon and unrolled a paper packet with the Color War teams and themes and officers!

"Omigod, omigod, omigod, omigod," she uttered in her head, but maybe also out loud. She was so excited and anxious and excited she couldn't tell! First, she noted the themes: Blue Psychedelic Sixties versus White Awesome Eighties. *Amazing.* Next, she noted the Blue Generals: counselors Ashanti Power and Jill McCarville, and the White Generals: counselors Jon Silver and Nicole Ferrara. *Quadruple amazing.* Third, she noted the Blue Lieutenants in her age group: Brian "Play Dough" Garfink and Bethany Melman. *OK, fine, whatever. No big surprise.* Fourth, she noted the White Lieutenants in her age group: Justin "Totle" Peterson and Jamie Nederbauer.

NOT OK, NOT FINE, NOT WHATEVER. Jamie? *Her* Jamie? Where was Jenny's name? She scanned the Lieutenant names under Notting Hill and Sherri Hill. Her name wasn't there, either. *This has got to be a joke. Or the world's worst mistake.* She flipped through the packet and found her name on the fourth page, on the Blue side, sandwiched between Melman and Sophie. No star. No title. Nothing. On the White side, Missi was sandwiched between Jamie and Slimey. Missi would be Jamie's second-in-command.

Jenny took a breath, but no air made it inside. The morning dew seemed to latch on to her skin. The sunrise felt like fire on her face. The camp erupted into a blur of cheers and screams and blues and whites, and Jenny couldn't move. She was on the brink of a breakdown.

blue Psychedelic 60s vs.

GENERALS

Ashanti Power

Jill McCarville

LIEUTENANTS

Hamburger Hill / Faith Hill

Brian “Play Dough” Garfink

Bethany Melman

Wawel Hill / Notting Hill

Alex Shale

Gabi Finkelstein

Highgate Hill / Sherri Hill

Elan Saad

Jasmine Figg

GENERALS

Jon Silver

Nicole Ferrara

LIEUTENANTS

Hamburger Hill / Faith Hill

Justin “Totle” Peterson

Jamie Nederbauer

Wawel Hill / Notting Hill

Timothy Wagner

Marti Kreitzer

Highgate Hill / Sherri Hill

David Burrick

Lauren Kasnett

COLOR WAR SCHEDULE

7:45 a.m.	Reveille
8:05 a.m.	Lineup
8:15 a.m.	Breakfast
8:45–9:25 a.m.	Cleanup/Inspection
9:30 a.m.	Team Lineup
9:35–10:45 a.m.	Activity Period A
10:55 a.m.–12:15 p.m.	Activity Period B
12:25 p.m.	Lunch Lineup
12:25–1:10 p.m.	Lunch
1:15–1:55 a.m.	Rest Hour
2:00 p.m.	Team Lineup
2:00–3:10 p.m.	Activity Period C
3:10 p.m.	Snack
3:30–4:45 p.m.	Activity Period D
4:45–6:00 p.m.	Dinner Prep
6:00 p.m.	Lineup
6:15–7:00 p.m.	Dinner
7:00–8:00 p.m.	Team Time
8:00 p.m.	Evening Activity
9:45 p.m.	Taps
10:00 p.m.–midnight	Officer meetings, SING prep

SPECIAL ACTIVITIES

DAY ONE

Breakout, Tug-o-War, Novelty Relays

DAY TWO

Bucket Brigade, Hatchet Hunt Introduction

DAY THREE

Apache Relay

DAY FOUR

Rope Burn

DAY FIVE

Mass Kickball, Marathon, Boating Regatta, Color Bowl

DAY SIX

Sealed Envelope Ceremony, SING

Tug-o-War

***"PSYCHO DELI!"* Play Dough cheered. He stood at the base of** Tennis Hill with his fellow Blue officers, facing his team for their first-ever meeting. He clapped twice at normal speed and then three times really fast. *"PSYCHO DELI!"* He was dressed in Wiener's blue basketball shorts and blue T-shirt. It was all so tight on him that his thighs pushed against the mesh shorts, and his arms ripped the shirt at the seams. He felt like the Hulk. Meanwhile, thirty feet away on Tennis Hill, where his opponents were assembled, Wiener was drowning in Play Dough's white stuff. They'd swapped clothes as soon as the war broke out, because Play Dough had assumed he'd be on White and Wiener had assumed he'd be on Blue, and they had both been dead wrong.

"PSYCHO DEL—"

"Lieutenant Play Dough!" General Ashanti Power stepped in front of Play Dough, halting him mid-cheer. He hovered over him like any counselor might, except that Ashanti Power was the opposite of most counselors, personality-wise. He wasn't chill or goofy; he'd graduated from JROTC, was going into his first year at the United States Merchant Marine Academy, and acted like a legit soldier even when it wasn't Color Wartime. A few weeks back, he'd sat On Duty for Hamburger Hill when Yoshi had his night off, and every time Play Dough farted, he'd made the whole bunk drop and give him twenty. Play Dough gave him twenty Pringles instead of push-ups, and Ashanti Power had crushed them all in his hand. The guy did not mess around. "What are you chanting, Lieutenant Play Dough?" he now barked.

"Uhhhh." General Power's intensity made Play Dough's mind go blank. Then his stomach rumbled and he remembered. "Psycho Deli, sir." He kicked his legs together military-style and smacked his inside anklebones. "Ow!"

"What is 'Psycho Deli'?" General Power asked.

Play Dough smiled. He wondered if General Power's saliva glands could handle his answer. "It's also known as the 'Psycho Chicken,'" he explained. "They sell it at Dheli's Deli on my corner at home. Fried chicken cutlet, bacon, avocado, pastrami—"

"Psy-che-del-ic," General Power annunciated. "Psychedelic."

"Ohhhhhhh," Play Dough said, as if "psychedelic" were a part of his everyday vocabulary, like, for example, the word "Muenster." "Sounds like a sandwich, but it's not!" He laughed it off.

"No, it's not a sandwich," General Power said with distaste, which Play Dough thought was pretty weird considering how tasty sandwiches are. "Psychedelic is mind-bending, tripping, out of this world."

So was a Psycho Chicken, but Play Dough wasn't about to say that. "Yeah, I know," he said instead, embarrassed.

"All righty then." General Power saluted and Play Dough saluted back. "It's time for the introductions. Can you get yourself together?"

Play Dough thought he was already together. But he followed General Power's eyes to his bare belly hanging out over the tight elastic of Wiener's shorts. *Stupid Wiener and his stupid muscle shirts*, Play Dough silently cursed. He stopped feeling like the Hulk. And he didn't feel smart like the Hulk's alter ego, Bruce Banner, either. Play Dough wished he hadn't exclusively worn all of his blue clothes last week to save up his white ones. He wished the Blue theme didn't remind him of a sandwich and mean something he still didn't understand. He wished Ashanti Power wasn't his General. He wished he was Lieutenant on White like the rest of his family had been.

Play Dough swallowed, stretched Wiener's shirt over his belly, and tried to put on a brave face. *You can do this*, he told himself. *You're Lieutenant! That's huge! Now all you have to do is lead your team to victory.*

General Power and General McCarville threw their fingers into a peace sign and swept the peace sign across their foreheads. *"Yodel, yodel, yodel, yodel, yodel, yodel-oo!"*

Play Dough and the other Lieutenants shouted back with the same peace sign move. *"Yodel, yodel, yodel, yodel, yodel, yodel-oo!"*

The Generals finished the chant: *"Groovy, hippie, Psychedelic Blue!"* They waved their arms in a fast motion like an umpire might to say, "Safe!" It cued silence.

"Hello, Blue team!" General Power shouted. He ran a hand

over his stubbly head and adjusted the blue leather bands he wore around his wrists. "I am Ashanti Power, Bunker Hill counselor and your General!" Everyone cheered, especially the Bunker Hillers. Play Dough had almost forgotten that the strictest staff member was in charge of the littlest kids. Apparently, they were all alive and well, so that was reassuring. "Together, we will accomplish one thing in this war: We will psychedelically slay the White! Please give it up for my co-General, the mighty flower child, hippie chick Jill McCarville!"

General McCarville spun around in a circle, tossing flower petals in the air. Her jeans flared over her Birks. A little dizzy, she put her hands around her mouth like a megaphone. "I am a Notting Hill counselor and your General, and together, my hippie tribe, we are going to obliterate the not-so-Awesome Eighties!" The Notting Hillers "woo"-ed the loudest of all the woo-ers.

Initiated by Lieutenant Melman, the Blue team did the wave. And then, led by the Wawel Hill Lieutenants, everyone did a "hippie dance," which involved moving around like each of your limbs was its own rubber snake. Play Dough noted it was pretty weird. But, being the leader he was, he rubber-snake danced. Until his shorts split.

Play Dough had split his shorts/pants before. It happened once when he was alone in his basement, playing Wii golf. So he'd just taken his sweats off and continued the game in his underwear. Another time, he was trying to do a split at a bar mitzvah to win a T-shirt with the DJ's name on it. He ended up winning the shirt, and being that it was an XXL, it went down to his knees, so no one noticed the hole in his crotch.

But this split was different. The shorts were torn from the top of Play Dough's butt crack all the way to the elastic waist in the front. He was basically wearing a mesh skirt. And Wiener's T-shirt was too small to cover all of his stomach rolls, let alone anything that far down. Play Dough crossed his legs and bent over to hide the tear, pretending to take the hippie dance to a new, weirder level. It seemed to work all right.

But then General Power quieted the team, and the dancing stopped, and Play Dough had to roll back up to standing so as to not look like he had problems. His priority was blocking the tear, though, so he kept his legs crossed and let his arms casually hover over his front. Then he tried to breathe through his nose to keep his face from turning the color of ketchup. General Power was saying stuff that Play Dough didn't hear, because he was too busy praying that the meeting would immediately terminate.

"Lieutenant Melman, you may begin!" was the first coherent thing he heard General Power say.

Uh-oh, Play Dough thought. *Begin what? 'Begin' is the opposite of 'terminate.'*

Melman leapt forward and threw her hands up. Play Dough hoped that movement would not be required of him. At this point, he wouldn't be able to untwist his legs or move his arms from his front without exposing himself.

"What's up, Blue team!" Melman shouted. "I'm Lieutenant Melman of Faith Hill Cabin, what-what!" She waved her bandana in the air and ruffled up her short blond hair that somehow already had streaks of blue in it. "I'm so pumped to Blue this week up!" After the team cheered for her, Melman looked back at Play Dough. When he didn't move, she waved at him to leap forward next to her and introduce himself.

Play Dough began to shake. Mostly because his twisted position was super-challenging to hold, like in Zumba, where his fitness-trainer mom dragged him once a week. She liked to start each class with a series of planks.

"Lieutenant Play Dough, is something wrong?" General Power asked in front of the whole team, which everyone knew was not what you were supposed to do to a kid in a split-shorts crisis.

"Uhhhh, nope."

"Do you want to introduce yourself?"

"Uhhhh, yup."

And that's when Play Dough remembered that he wasn't in Zumba with really fit stay-at-home moms or at a bar mitzvah with skinny punks. He was at camp, where there was a different definition of cool. Maybe split shorts would become the new Color War dress code. He'd heard his dad talk about wanting a president he could, in theory, grab a beer with. Well, maybe his team wanted a Lieutenant they could, in theory, hang out with in their underwear. He leapt forward and threw his arms up like he'd seen Melman do.

Wiener's shirt tore at Play Dough's pits. The shorts split through the elastic and fell down to his ankles. The team roared with laughter. Play Dough hammed it up, sniffing his armpit holes and doing the rubbery-snake dance again in nothing but his tighty-whities and torn T-shirt. "I'm Lieutenant Play Dough, and I'm a hippie who doesn't like being confined by clothes!"

In the crowd, Play Dough spotted his teammates Smelly and Dover waving tie-dyed streamers over their heads, laughing hysterically. Play Dough felt like a hippied-out Hulk and Bruce Banner wrapped in one!

He tried to find Jenny, excited to see her pretty, proud smile. He could only imagine how very impressed she was right now. Her friend was Lieutenant and killing it! He finally spotted her beside a blue-wigged Sophie. Jenny's face was the pink of tomato cream sauce and her eyes were puffy like pumpernickel mini-bagels. She did not look entertained. She looked miserable.

And then, something totally unexpected happened. Someone in the crowd yelled, "Traitor!" and another yelled, "Blue betrayer!" Play Dough had no idea why. It crossed his mind that he wasn't the only one aware of his family history on the White team. Or maybe his teammates were upset he'd torn up his blue clothes? As *"Traitor, traitor, Blue betrayer"* became a chant on repeat, the Highgate and Sherri Hill Lieutenants approached Play Dough, holding a bucket of something. They pointed at his tighty-*whities*, shook their heads, and splashed his underwear area with blue paint. It was cold and sticky and hardened against his clothes and skin.

Play Dough tried to keep a smile stuck on his face and go along with the whole gag, but his insides were all knotted up. He didn't like being called a traitor or a Blue betrayer. He didn't like being naked-ish in front of everyone. He didn't like getting paint thrown on him or how the paint chipped at the fatty parts of his belly. He didn't like that Jenny had her face buried in her hands and not in a *I can't stop laughing at my hilarious friend* way.

Play Dough then caught a glimpse of General Power, his face twisted in confusion. "All right," Power said, raising his fingers in a peace sign to hush the crowd. "Acting stupid does not a war hero make." He cocked his chin at Lieutenant Finkelstein to step forward and introduce herself. She did, keeping her distance from Play Dough and all the wet paint.

Play Dough then had to stand there in the line of officers for what felt like the longest Zumba class in the world. Without even looking to his left, he could feel the Awesome Eighties team cutting glances at him, curious about all the commotion. And he could feel the Blue team not really paying attention to the other Blue officers and their introductions. How could they when they had a blue-painted fatty to snicker at?

Play Dough was pretty sure standing naked-ish in front of a crowd, without being able to make a joke of it, was an ancient torture technique. He feared he looked deranged as he fought to keep his smile plastered to his face, so he let it go and made himself look serious. But he only ever looked serious when he was angry, and he wasn't angry, exactly. More like he thought he might crumble.

Luckily, the meeting eventually ended, and the Captain and TJ announced that it was time for the very first Color War event: Tug-o-War! The Generals were called on to set up the rope that stretched from one corner of the net-free tennis court to the other, while the Lieutenants were left in charge to lead their teams in more cheers. At which point, one of the older, bigger girls threw Play Dough a pair of her shorts. He put them on, unsure if the extra six inches of fabric down his thigh made him look any less like a fat moron. He led his team with: "B-B-L, B-L-U-E, Blue team to victory!" and tried to transfer all of his embarrassed energy into just being really loud.

The Captain tapped the mic three times. "Blue and White Lieutenants, please join your Generals on the court. Lieutenants will tug. Generals will motivate." Play Dough was aware that "motivate" meant that the Generals would be running up and down the rope, screaming in their officers' faces. He knew what was up. He'd seen this happen from Tennis Hill four summers in a row.

The Captain continued: "Psychedelic Sixties on the left and Awesome Eighties on the right." Play Dough's brain short-circuited between pumped-up excitement and residual embarrassment that he was wearing girl shorts. *No one will think I'm a fat moron after this*, Play Dough assured himself, taking his place as anchor, the position at the end of the rope reserved for the heaviest teammate.

Play Dough checked out the Highgate Hill White Lieutenant who was anchoring opposite him. Play Dough estimated that he had about eighteen pounds on his opponent. This was going to be as easy as pie. Or more like as easy as cereal, because pie was actually pretty hard to get right.

Play Dough looked out at the rest of the Blue team, standing on top of Tennis Hill, clapping and cheering. *After this tug I'll be a fat hero!* he told himself, smiling for real. *Just you wait.*

General Power had his hands on his knees, whispering strategy to Lieutenant Melman, who was first in line, also a very important position. Then he headed straight for Play Dough and bent down in the same hands-on-knees position. Play Dough was ready for whatever "motivation" he was about to get. Even his belly rolls hardened with confidence.

"Lieutenant Play Dough," General Power said, "we both know you tend to act silly for attention." Play Dough didn't think that was true. He acted *funny* for attention, because one day he'd be a stand-up comedian. Or a lawyer who made everyone, including the whole jury, roar with laughter. "Silly" was what his little sister was when she tried to feed her dolls to their cats.

Suddenly, Play Dough realized General Power was waiting for him to nod in agreement, so he did, just to get the pep talk over with. Then, as if being called "silly" wasn't hurtful enough, General Power proceeded with a fat-person dig: "It's not every sport that the heavier you are the more power you have."

Play Dough couldn't resist delivering a comedian-worthy comeback. "Well, there's sumo wrestling and hot dog eating and bowling, if you're the ball." *Boom! Silly, my butt!*

General Power just stared at him, the joke going right over his military buzz cut.

"Sorry," Play Dough croaked.

"The anchor holds all of the power. Don't let us down."

"I won't," Play Dough said, kicking his legs together again.

TJ tapped the mic. "All right, everybody, listen up." The teams went quiet, in fear of losing any points. Play Dough checked out the Captain standing center court, holding the exact middle of the rope marked by blue and white duct tape. There was a large chalk circle drawn at her feet. Whichever team pulled the rope so that the duct-taped middle made it over the chalk circle to their side first, won! Play Dough wouldn't be able to see the chalk from where he was, all the way in the back, so he reminded himself to just keep pulling until the Captain blew her whistle and announced a Blue victory.

TJ carried on: "The winning team of each major Color War activity is awarded a Sealed Envelope, which contains a mysterious, predetermined amount of points ranging from zero to five hundred. The winner of Tug-o-War will get the first Sealed Envelope of the summer. Sealed Envelopes will be opened the last day of the war. Any questions?" When no one made a sound, TJ lowered his voice, trying to sound extra-intense for the war. "Please pick up the rope."

Play Dough picked up the end of the rope, wrapped it around his middle like he'd seen all of the anchors before him do, and bent his knees.

"Remember," General McCarville whispered down the line, "the best strategy is looking up and pulling extra hard on three." The Lieutenants nodded, ready to do just that. Play Dough looked up at the sky. Normally, it was so blue. Today, there were whipped-cream clouds. This was not a good omen.

TJ boomed into the mic: "On your marks, get set . . ." He held the mic to the Captain's mouth, where a whistle was resting between her lips. She blew.

The teams went wild: *"P-U-L-L, pull the rope! P-U-L-L, pull the rope!"*

Play Dough leaned back as hard as he could. In no time, General Power was in his face, screaming: "One, two, PUUULL!" Play Dough pulled just enough on the "One, two" so that his team didn't trip forward, and then pulled extra hard on "PUUULL."

For a while, probably ten seconds, both teams were at a standstill. Blue shuffled back and then White shuffled back, but no team was making real progress. Then, miraculously, White must have gotten tired and Blue must have gotten Hulk-ier, because Blue made huge strides back! Blue's cheering soared. General Power's eyes lit up like a bonfire.

Then Play Dough started to sweat. He felt it bead on his neck and forehead. He felt it on his palms as the rope slipped a little through his fingers. He felt it dampen his chest. He felt it drip down to his belly, around where the rope was. The chipping paint near his waist turned gloopy. Suddenly, the rope was gliding through the gloop around his middle. He didn't have time to wait to pull extra hard on "PUUULL." He needed to pull now, as hard as possible. So he did. The rope slipped, spinning him twice around like a not-yet-dry, not-yet-ready dreidel.

Play Dough watched it all like an out-of-body experience. First, he teetered backward and fell on his butt. He might have split his girl shorts. And then all of his Lieutenants skidded forward. Their faces contorted like they were constipated. They tried leaning back and looking up at a sky of white, but they just tripped over their feet and moved closer and closer to White's side. The White team roared, "Awesome Eighties! Awesome Eighties!" and General Power's eyes went from bonfire-bright to charcoal-scary. "PUUUUUULLL!!!!" he growled.

But it was too late. Melman stumbled toward her opponents, and the duct-taped middle of the rope surpassed its chalk boundary. The Captain blew her whistle and motioned to White for the win.

Both teams dropped the rope. The White officers began jumping up and down. Lieutenants Totle and Jamie hugged. General Silver and General Ferrara performed the moonwalk, and up on Tennis Hill, the White team waved neon streamers and sang, *"We're electric, boogie-woogie, woogie!"* Meanwhile, General Power paced to the edge of the court, trying to collect himself. The Blue team hung their heads and clapped weakly. "We'll get 'em next time," General McCarville said. Jenny had disappeared.

Melman began huddling up the Blue officers, probably for a dumb, reinspiration speech, but Play Dough didn't budge from the corner where he'd fallen. He had his legs out straight, afraid to check if the girl shorts had actually split. The blue paint had started to drip dry and crack around his belly again.

"Hey, Lieutenant Play Dough, you joining us?" she asked, smiling through her disappointment like a pro.

Play Dough didn't want to be pathetic and say, "No, my shorts might be split again," or "I don't deserve to join the huddle because losing Tug-o-War was all my fault," so he just shrugged and said, "Nah."

General Power strode back toward the huddle. He paused when he reached Play Dough and took a breath, like he was going to deliver a pep talk, but then he just sighed really loud, like *Why bother?*

CAMP ROCKS!

Date: August 12

Dear Uncle Frank, Aunt Gillian, Jess, Drew, and Sparky,

How are you? I am Color War Lieutenant!!! OMG it's insane. I'm on White Awesome. '80s. were u alive then?
Camp is totally tubular, no duh!
.

Today we won Tug-o-War because Lt. Play Dough's painted tummy made the rope slip, hahahaha, lol.
My favorite thing so far is W-H-I-T-E, White team to victory!!!!!!!.

My cabin is where I write all the activity rosters because im the boss of everything .
The food is was blue and white pancakes yesterday. Now it's normal colors.
Write back soon!

From,
Lt. Nederbauer

August 12

Dear Journal,

Today is a most fortunate day. I am a Color War Lieutenant.

It is important to me that I lead the White team to victory, using my original STARFISH values system, with one tweak.

S is for Sportsmanship.

Shake hands after games, no matter what.

T is for Tolerance.

Tolerate the Blue team even if they don't shake hands.

A is for Appreciation. Admiration. Awesome.

Always remember how Awesome the Eighties are.

R is for Respect.

Respect the rules or else the Captain will take points away.

F is for Friendship.

Find the Color War Hatchet with your friends.

I is for Integrity.

I still don't remember what this one means.

S is for Sensitivity.

Don't cry if you lose one dumb activity.

H is for Helpfulness.

Help your team win.

"There's no war that will end all wars."
—Haruki Murakami
(a famous Japanese writer who might be related to Steinberg)

I like this quote because once this Color War is over, there will be another Color War next summer. It never ends!

"Raw" is "War" spelled backward,
Totle

12 August

Dear Little Ealing Fireflies,

Whassup? Things on this side of the pond have been a bit crazy. Color War broke out, and it's almost as competitive as our rivalry with the Mulberry Munks. I'm Lieutenant for the Psychedelic '60s team, and I'm trying to lead Coach Sully–style. Or like how you lead, Captain Mary Banks. Anyway, you're both my inspiration.

Fun fact: Pelé was in his prime in the 1960s, so I think the theme is meant to be :)

Kick butt, always.

#24,
Melman

August 12th

Dear Gramps,

Call Pops and Great-Uncle Garfink and Aunt Denise, and tell them the news . . .

Lt. Garfink in the HOUUUUUUUUSE!

I'm fist-bumping you potato French fries-style through this letter. (That's when you make a fist like a potato and after you bump it, you explode your fingers out like fries.)

Here's the thing, though. I'm on Blue, not White like you and everyone else in the Garfink family. I know, I know, I'm sorry. It stinks worse than farts.

But seriously, I think it's kind of messing with my head. I keep doing dumb stuff that's costing my team points. I need luck real bad.

Any advice for your crazy grandson? I could use a little lovin'.

Thank you,
Brian

NOVELTY RELAYS

Sewing Relay. A large spoon is tied to a spool of yarn. Standing in a line, the campers sew themselves together: down one person's shirt and shorts, up the next person's shirt and shorts. *Your parents will thank us for teaching you this skill.*

Egg Toss. Toss the egg to your partner. Both then take a step back. Repeat until egg breaks. *DO NOT EAT THE EGG. We will feed you cooked food later if you're hungry.*

Sneaker Relay. Campers' sneakers are mixed together in a heaping pile. At the whistle, each camper must find their sneakers, put them on, and tie the laces. *Velcro is a no-go!*

Scooter Relay. One camper rides the scooter; the other pushes him or her the length of the court. *Protect your fingers. This is how fingers get lost!*

Hula-Hooping. Hula-Hoop until it hits the floor. No hands. *Or hips. Just kidding.*

Shuttle Relay. Sprint back and forth, picking up and dropping blocks halfway down the court. *We will have inhalers on site. Thanks to Steinberg for the generous donation.*

Frozen T-shirt Contest. Each officer is given one completely frozen folded T-shirt. Thaw it! The first team with all of their shirts on (arms through), wins. *Hypothermia is a risk, but one worth taking.*

How to Unfreeze a T-Shirt in Seven Obvious Steps

In and out and in and out and in and out and in.

Jenny watched the Sewing Relay from the basketball bleachers in the exact same spot she'd sat yesterday when she was contemplating her Lieutenantship with Play Dough. There he was now, on the basketball court, under the bug-swarming lights, threading yarn from the bottom of his sweats up through the top of his T-shirt, living out his dream. And there on the opposite side of the court was Jamie, threading yarn from the top of her T-shirt to the bottom of her velour sweats, living out Jenny's dream.

Ever since the war broke out fifteen hours ago, Jamie had been giving Jenny the silent treatment. She hadn't comforted Jenny. Or apologized for stealing Jenny's dream. Or reassured Jenny that the Color War packets had a major typo. Instead, Jamie had soaked up the glory that came with being Lieutenant, ignoring the fact that this was obviously a case of mistaken identity.

During Rest Hour, Jamie had Missi face-paint AWESOME '80s on her forehead, and paint her nails white, and cover her stringy hair with baby powder. Meanwhile, Jenny'd had no one to help her Blue herself up—Melman had been busy writing rosters for the Novelty Relays, and Sophie had been listening to the soundtrack of *Hair* for Psychedelic Sixties research. Jenny wondered if Jamie knew that the baby powder made her look like she was celebrating her eightieth birthday and not the 1980s. Normally, she'd tell her Best Friend that she was a fashion disaster, but not now when things were so awkward between them. If Jamie wanted to look like a senile grandma, then that was her problem.

Jamie pulled the giant spoon from her pant leg and held it above her head. Then Lieutenant Totle, who was standing beside her in the relay, twirled her in celebration. Jenny had never seen Jamie twirled by anyone besides her. She'd never imagined Jamie could have that much fun without her. That Jamie could do so well without her help. Jenny felt her heart pinch.

As with all Color War activities, just in case there was a disqualification or a penalty, both teams had to finish what they'd started. So, last in line, Melman threaded the yarn up through her shirt, cheering as if it actually mattered: "Almost, almost, almost!"

Jenny wanted to scream. "Almost" was the word of a loser. Almost winners were losers. Almost Lieutenants were title-free nothings.

Melman unyarned herself, and the Captain blew her whistle. "The Sewing Relay goes to . . . WHITE!" White screamed.

Yay, awesome job, Jenny thought sarcastically.

"Jenny, you're up!" Melman called as she jogged off the court.

"Up for what?" Jenny asked.

"Egg Toss!"

Jenny bulged her eyes. She wasn't flattered; she was mortified. "What about Sophie?"

Jenny and Melman looked at Sophie. "I don't believe in the abuse of eggs for entertainment," Sophie said. "I find it very uncivilized. But if it's going to happen one way or another, I would like to be the one to toss and protect." She gave a three-finger salute, à la Katniss Everdeen in *The Hunger Games*.

Melman winced regretfully. "I didn't know you felt so passionately about it."

What?! How had Melman not known? Was she selectively deaf to Sophie's extensive chats about Duckie, Sondra, and Namaste Edgersteckin, her three egg babies? Had Melman blocked out Sophie's story about how some deranged monster-bully in the cafeteria had chucked Namaste at her head? Sophie had caught the poor, egg-napped baby in the taco-meat pile on her tray! She should be competing in the Egg Toss, a no-brainer.

Melman continued, relentlessly upbeat. "The good news, Soph, is that I have you down for the Sneaker Relay!"

"That's a problem." She stuck out her Velcro sandal. "I'm not wearing sneakers, and I'm a size nine. I can't borrow. Your feet are too small."

Jenny rolled her eyes at Sophie's blatant unpreparedness and Melman's lack of common sense in her assignment of events.

Melman nodded at Sophie's foot. "But you know what, J?" Jenny braced herself for whatever dumb motivational line Melman was about to vomit. "You're going to toss it out of the egg park!" There it was.

Jenny ignored Melman and took her place on the court opposite Smelly, while the other pairs took their places beside them. Jenny was losing herself in Smelly's nervous eyes, thinking about the fact that they'd be tossing an egg until it met its demise. Then they'd lose. Suddenly, Jenny was struck with an idea! She'd learned from *Pretty Little Liars* that when assailants learn their victim's name, it pulls on their heartstrings and makes them reconsider murder. "What should we name her?" she asked Smelly.

"Huh?" Smelly asked.

"The egg," Jenny said. "Naming her will naturally motivate us to keep her from cracking to death."

"Uh, how 'bout 'Eggy'?" Smelly suggested.

Yes, Eggy. That's a very sympathetic name, Jenny thought sarcastically. This egg was going to die.

The Captain tapped the mic. "Attention, Blue and White. Before we begin, please note: Eggs will crack. Participants, DO NOT eat the cracked eggs. They are uncooked and WILL give you salmonella."

General Power leaned into the mic. "That means you, Lieutenant Play Dough. We all know you'll put anything with a calorie in your mouth."

Both teams cracked up. Play Dough waved at the chuckling crowd like a true sport, but Jenny could tell he was embarrassed—his cheeks turned pink and his eyes glazed over. Sure, Play Dough liked food, but he wasn't the idiot General Power kept making him out to be. That was another reason this Color War needed Jenny to lead—she'd stand up for her fellow officers instead of blindly focusing on the positive like Melman was doing.

"You may TOSS your EGG!" the Captain announced.

Jenny hopped to attention. Smelly lobbed Eggy to her. The shell smacked her inner knuckles but didn't crack. Jenny gently lobbed Eggy to Smelly. Too short, but Smelly dove to save her. Jenny wished they had a concrete strategy. She looked at Sophie for help, but Sophie was wearing her sweatshirt backward, the hood up over her face. This was all too much for her to stand. And it was all too much for Jenny to stand, too. Eggs were splatting left and right. Smelly lobbed Eggy to Jenny. Jenny caught Eggy against her stomach. She lobbed Eggy to Smelly. Too far, but Smelly sprinted backward and caught her over some Bunker Hiller's lap.

"Nice catch, Smelly!" Melman cheered. "See? You can do it, Jenny! You can really throw and catch!"

Jenny cringed. Of course she could throw and catch. Was she the only one who knew she was athletic? Just because she didn't want to play sports ALL THE TIME like Melman did didn't mean she was an uncoordinated Barbie or whatever. But it also didn't mean she had what it took to be in the last Egg Toss pair standing—so far, every back and forth had been a miracle.

Jenny looked down the court at Missi and Wiener, who were doing a lot of exaggerated lunging and cradling—they seemed to be doing all right. Maybe she could adopt their strategy. She practiced a lunge. And then she felt a splat against her chest. There was egg yolk dripping down her body. Eggy had died. "You're supposed to make eye contact!" she yelled at Smelly. "I wasn't ready. Hellooooo!"

"Sorry," Smelly said. "I couldn't tell. You're wearing sunglasses."

Jenny had forgotten. She'd thrown them on before lunch to hide her swollen-from-crying eyes and had apparently kept them on long after the sun had set. "We should have named our egg something beautiful," Jenny told him, moving the sunglasses to the top of her head. "Like 'Isabella Ryan.'" That was Jenny's all-time favorite name. It would be the name of her first-born baby or puppy, whichever came first. "With a name like Isabella Ryan, you would have been more careful."

"I liked 'Eggy.'"

"No you didn't."

"Uh, OK."

Jenny tended to have a kind of power over people—the kind that got them to agree with her, which was the billionth reason she would have made an amazing Lieutenant. Simply put, Melman was too nice. There was no room for niceness in war. It was how eggs died, and points were lost, and Sealed Envelopes were forfeited to the enemy.

The Captain boomed into the mic: "The Egg Toss goes to . . . WHITE!"

Jenny looked down the court at Missi and Wiener, who were holding hands and jumping up and down. Their dumb, nameless egg baby was being Simba'd by Totle for all of White to worship. Then Jenny watched as Jamie leapt onto Missi and covered her with a million kisses. Laughing hysterically, the girls fell to the ground and rolled on top of cracked eggs. It was gross.

Jenny felt her heart go all runny like yolk, and threw her sunglasses back down over her eyes. She wished Christopher were here. He'd lift her high in the sky à la *Dirty Dancing* and yell at Melman, "No one puts Jenny in the Egg Toss!" Then they'd hold hands and kiss and he'd assure Jenny that she was too good to be Lieutenant. She was too pretty and too smart and too athletic and too amazing.

Since Melman hadn't assigned Jenny to any more events, Jenny offered to chart the results for the rest of the Novelty Relays. Melman didn't seem to think she'd need the results for her records, since the judges kept track of everything, but Jenny knew from recent past experience that TJ and the Captain were privy to making errors. (Cough, cough, not making Jenny a Lieutenant.) Plus, Jenny probably had salmonella festering on her shirt and could use the distraction. Relay after relay, she wrote down the competitors and the winner.

EVENT/RELAY	BLUE Faith/Hamburger Competitors	WHITE Faith/Hamburger Competitors	WINNER
Sewing Relay	Melman & Play Dough (officers only)	Jamie & Totle (officers only)	White
Egg Toss	Jenny & Smelly	Missi & Wiener	White
Sneaker Relay	Sophie (with PD's sneakers) & Dover	Slimey & Steinberg	Blue
Scooter Relay	Melman & Smelly	Missi & Totle	Blue
Hula Hooping	Sophie & Play Dough	Jamie & Wiener	White
Shuttle Relay	Melman & Dover	Slimey & Wiener	Blue
Frozen T-shirt Contest	Melman & Play Dough (officers only)	Jamie & Totle (officers only)	

After Blue took home the Shuttle Relay, the Captain tapped the mic to hush the crowd. “Bravo and brava, Blue and White! We have one last event for tonight’s Novelty Relays: the Frozen T-shirt Contest!” There were a bunch of extra-loud cheers. The Frozen T-shirt Contest was by far the best, most exciting, event of the Novelty Relays. It was also the event that Jenny had studied the hardest. The Captain carried on: “Each officer will be given a frozen T-shirt. The officers’ job is to unfreeze their shirt just enough so that they can wear it, arms and head through all the right holes. The first team to have all of their shirts on wins!”

As fast as lightning, Jenny scribbled strategies on the back of the score chart:

HOW TO WIN THE FROZEN T-SHIRT CONTEST

(1) Find a puddle. Immerse your T-shirt.
(2) Hog the water fountain. Run water over your T-shirt.
(3) Spit on your T-shirt. Suck on a lemon to get the saliva going.
(4) Wack your T-shirt against the basketball poles.
(5) Wack your T-shirt against the courtside light poles.

(6) Climb the light pole and hold your T-shirt up to the bulb.

(7) As a last, gross resort, pee on your T-shirt.

Jenny wanted to relay these strategies to Melman, but Melman was already huddled up with the Blue officers. She thought about slipping the info to Play Dough, who was getting a drink of water, but by the time she reached the fountain, he'd be huddled up, too. Running thin on ideas, she turned to Sophie.

"Sophster." Sophie was still shaken up by the eggs (literally, she was shaking), so Jenny tried to be extra-sensitive. "Do you think Melman knows how to unfreeze a T-shirt?"

"Probably."

"She doesn't."

"If you knew the answer, then—?"

"Because I *do* know how to unfreeze a T-shirt. And I know how to do it better than anyone else." Jenny offered Sophie the paper and watched her read the strategies in two seconds flat.

The Captain continued into the mic: "Since both Blue and White have three wins, the winner of the Frozen T-shirt Contest will earn the second Sealed Envelope of the war!"

"We're tied, Sophie," Jenny said, flipping over the paper to the chart. "So it's über-important that Melman knows what she's doing. We need to get her this paper."

Before Jenny could say another word, Sophie began a weird origami project, folding the paper into an elephant—no—a

Dutch hat—no—an airplane! "Omigod, you're a genius!" Jenny squealed.

Sophie threw the paper airplane across the court. It soared toward Melman, but at the very last second swooped down and over, crashing into the back of Jamie's head.

Jenny full-body cringed as she watched Jamie rub her hair, spot the paper airplane at her feet, look around in massive confusion, and then unfold it. "No, no, no, no, no!" Jenny muttered under her breath.

"My bad," Sophie mumbled. She put her hood back up over her face.

On the court, TJ rolled out a cooler of frozen T-shirts. "I froze the shirts under the birthday ice cream three weeks ago. They're rock-solid." He lifted the cover—the ice was so cold, it was gassing up before the officers' eyes. Jamie was so absorbed in Jenny's strategies, she didn't even seem to notice.

"Ready, set . . . UNFREEZE!" the Captain called.

Jenny watched with horror as Play Dough approached his T-shirt with his tongue. "Spit, Play Dough, you're supposed to spit!" she yelled from the bleachers. But it was too late. Play Dough's tongue suctioned to his shirt. Then Melman neglected her shirt to help Play Dough detach himself. *Too nice.*

Meanwhile, Jamie had her shirt immersed in a courtside puddle and was shouting at her fellow officers: "Wack it! Wet it! Bring it to the light!" They were doing just as she said. Jamie had never looked so competent in her life.

Jenny wished she could take credit for her ideas. But she and Sophie would be thought of as traitors. Jenny already had egg yolk hardening on her clothes. She didn't also need blue paint thrown on her, like how the officers had done to Play Dough.

Ten minutes later, all eight White officers were wearing their unfrozen T-shirts, and only six of the Blue officers were wearing theirs. Play Dough's tongue was finally free, but he and Melman were super-behind in the T-shirt unfreezing department. And so, protocol being protocol, both teams had to watch for five more minutes until they finally got their shirts over their heads. Then TJ blew his whistle, and without even saying it aloud, the Captain whooshed her arms to White.

The White team erupted: "Ne-der-bau-er! Ne-der-bau-er!"

Jenny could barely process the fact that half the camp was screaming for Jamie, and the other half was probably wishing she'd been assigned to Blue.

Jamie lifted her velour pants so they wouldn't drag on the ground and pranced over to Jenny with a huge smile. Jenny froze in terror as Jamie threw her arms around her neck and whispered: "I recognized your handwriting! Omigod, thank you, thank you!"

Jenny peeled Jamie off of her. Jamie was on White. She was a Lieutenant. Didn't she know that embracing Jenny, that *thanking* Jenny, was *so not OK*? "For what?" Jenny asked, trying to play it cool.

"For the—" She stopped herself and pulled Jenny's list from her pocket. "I'm so relieved. I thought you were mad at me all day today!"

Inside, Jenny stumbled a little. She *had* been mad at Jamie.

But admitting that would be admitting a whole bunch of other stuff she didn't want to admit. "Why would I be mad at you?" Jenny asked.

Jamie shrunk at the shoulders. "Um. Because I'm Lieutenant and you're not."

Well, that's dumb, Jenny thought. Jamie should have asked her if they were on OK terms instead of assuming that they weren't and walking around like God's gift to camp. But Jenny didn't want to seem needy or resentful. So she lied. "I'm not mad at you," she said. "I'm scared for you."

"Is that why you air-dropped me help?" Jamie asked, trying to understand.

Jenny's lies seemed to be piecing together nicely, so she decided to keep at it. "Yeah," she said. "I helped you, because without me you'd just embarrass yourself."

"Oh," Jamie said.

"Yeah," Jenny confirmed. "Sorry, but it's true."

Jamie squinted in thought. And then said meekly, "I thought I was doing OK on my own. I was sort of proud of myself."

Jenny thought back to the full day of activities they'd had, from Tug-o-War to volleyball to tennis to the Novelty Relays. Jamie had been spirited and organized. She'd led her team to victory on more than one occasion. She actually deserved to be proud of herself. But now was not the time for compliments. Admitting Jamie's success was admitting that camp didn't need Jenny to lead a team, after all. That the position she'd been striving for really could go to any Upper Camper. That Jenny's destiny was possibly nothing special. So Jenny did the only thing she could think of. She laughed. A really mean, nasty laugh.

"You know what?" Jamie said, tossing her skinny arms up. "You're just jealous. And yeah, maybe you would have made a really good Lieutenant, but no one asked you to be one. They asked me. And so far, I'm doing awesome. I don't need any more of your help." She tossed Jenny her airplane of strategies and scores. "In fact, you've been trying to keep me in your shadow for four summers, and I realize now that, without you, I'm a bigger, better person! Bigger and better than you!"

Jenny was glad that she had her sunglasses on. She was not glad that the sunglasses didn't extend to her chin, where a tear was sliding. She caught the tear with the back of her hand and then rubbed her chin like she was deep in thought and not losing control of her emotions. "Yeah, well, you look like a grandma with your hair like that," she told Jamie.

"And you look like a loser," Jamie fired back. "A mean, eggy, no-one-cares-about-you LOSER."

August 13

Dear Duckie, Sondra, and Namaste,

What up—what up—what up, my eggs-ellent babies! Oh, how glad I am that you are safe at home on my desk and not cracked on the basketball court, collateral damage to a war you're not even fighting.

On the sunny-side up, Color War is otherwise fun! Today, we had the Bucket Brigade. What's the Bucket Brigade, you ask? YOU DON'T KNOW?!?!

Of course you don't. You're eggs.

The Bucket Brigade: The two teams line up from the lake's dock to the peak of Forest Hill, passing pitchers of lake water to an empty laundry bin. First team to get their bin to overflow wins!

And guess what?! BLUE WON!

Let the sunshine in,
Sophie Edgersteckin
aka your eggs-traordinary mama hen

CAMP ROCKS!

August 13

Dear li'l bro,

Color War just keeps getting better and better. Yesterday Missi (my first kiss/GF, probably) and I owned the Egg Toss. Also known as WE WON IT.

Top secret scoop: It's all about the curtsey lunge.

I guess you could say we're a couple of egg-savers.

Catch you soon, baby yolk.

Your big bro (Egg Toss pro),
Ernie

August 13th

Dear Mom,

How are you? Color War's amazing!!! I'm on White Awesome Eighties and it's so AWESOME because we get to wear neon clothes off the shoulder and do Richard Simmons dance moves!! So cheesy, but so fun ☺.

Jamie's my Lieutenant, and she's doing an amazing job. It's so inspiring seeing her step up to the plate and lead her team like a B-O-S-S! Even though I'm separated from Bobby and Melman (she's Lieutenant for Blue!!!), it's cool because I get to hang out with Missi and Jamie, who otherwise I might not spend a lot of time with. Color War is just the greatest for that reason.

Tell Lois she's a totally rad cockatiel! (That's an '80s saying—there are so many that make me laugh! Haha!)

Love,
Stephanie

Hey, Jenny,

Wat up? You're a kewl kat but I think we should break up.

So stop being my girlfriend when you read this.

Congrats on being a lootenant on the blue and white team.

Chris

Lake Bread for the Teenage Soul

Play Dough was sitting on a life jacket inside a canoe inside the Boat Shack, munching on white bread, and he couldn't have been more relieved. Lunch had ended an hour ago and snack wasn't until 3:10 P.M., and if General Power thought Play Dough could wait that long, he was high on Cheez Whiz. Leading a team used a lot of energy. Leading a team poorly and getting called out for it used up even more. He could tell by the sweatfall of his pits. This week, it had reached a record high.

TJ's voice blared from the corner of the shack. Play Dough jolted forward.

> **TJ:** Good afternoon, Rolling Hills! The time has come to talk about one of Color War's biggest events. It rhymes with Ratchet Stunt. Can anyone guess what it is? [*singing the* Jeopardy *theme song*] *Do, do, do, do—*
>
> **Captain:** TJ, we don't have a lot of time.
>
> **TJ:** The Hatchet Hunt!
>
> **Captain:** Every summer we hide the Color War Hatchet on the campgrounds.

TJ: But not in any cabins! Maybe *under* a cabin or *around* a cabin, but certainly not *inside* of one.

Captain: No private spaces—they understand.

TJ: Past hiding spots include: The Dining Hall chimney. Backstage, inside the papier-mâché hill for the Fourth of July show. And my favorite, the toilet of the Social Hall unisex bathroom.

Captain: We don't repeat hiding spots, so save yourself time and don't look there.

TJ: Other toilets, though—knock yourself out.

Captain: The Hatchet is not in any toilet. Please don't go reaching inside toilets.

TJ: Then where should they look, Captain?

Captain: We have clues for you. Two clues will be announced per day until the Hatchet is found.

Say a clue now! Play Dough thought back to past clues. When the Hatchet was hidden in the Dining Hall chimney, the clue was "Longest word in English," which led campers to "Supercalifragilisticexpialidocious," which led them to *Mary Poppins*, which led them to chimney sweeps, which led them to the chimney. That one was easy. The clues for the toilet-bound Hatchet were really hard. The first clue was "Crib Lay Age" which is "Glacier Bay" scrambled, which is a national park in Alaska, which is irrelevant. The relevant part: Glacier Bay is a brand of toilet, the kind that the Hatchet was hidden inside.

The Hatchet Hunt was Play Dough's favorite part of Color War. He was subpar in athletics, had subpar brainpower, and was only good-par at art stuff that required stick figures, but, oh boy, was he adventurous. Chimney climbing? Scenery destruction? Toilet digging? Sign him up. Plus, Play Dough bet finding the Hatchet would make up for all the dumb mistakes he'd made so far. He could see it in the headline of the *Hilltopper*, Camp Rolling Hills' only online blog: "Lieutenant Garfink, a Blue Pioneer and Hatcheteer! Not a Fat Moron, No Sir!"

TJ: The very first clue is . . . Wait for it—
Captain: *Lady and the Tramp.*

That Disney dog movie from sixty years ago? Play Dough's mind was already spinning with hiding spots. He dissected the word "Disney." Disney ➡ dis-knee ➡ this knee ➡ when your knee hurts you go to the infirmary = the steps of the infirmary! He then dissected the word "dog." Dog ➡ *woof! ruff!* ➡ sounds like "roof" = the roof of any cabin! He would have to narrow that down a bit more.

TJ: And when can teams search for the Hatchet?
Captain: Wonderful question, TJ. The Hatchet can only be hunted an hour before reveille, during Rest Hour, and during Free Play. All other times are off-limits.
TJ: So, basically, no ditching your activities to go looky-looky. But, if you *find* the Hatchet at your activity, that's fair game. What happens once the Hatchet is found?
Captain: Another stellar question. The answer is: Bring it to us. In exchange, your team will earn a Sealed Envelope.

TJ: This summer, the Hatchet is worth—!

Captain: You'll have to wait to see.

The loudspeaker went off with a sharp squeal.

Worth how much?! Play Dough couldn't believe he'd have to wait four more days to find out. He thought back to previous Color Wars. The Hatchet had never been worth less than sixty points and never more than two hundred, which, compared to activities like the Novelty Relays, which were worth thirty to eighty points, was a lot. The hunt was on.

Suddenly, the door of the Boat Shack began to rattle and then burst open, ripping Play Dough from his Hatchet dreaming. "I'm putting the fishing rods away!" he cried. "Hold on, I'm just—!" He frantically looked up at the boobs hovering above him. "Oh, it's you." He wanted to sigh with relief, but Jenny was no less intimidating than who he'd thought it was. Just more hot.

"Who'd you think it was?" she asked.

Uh, General Power. It would be just like him to catch Play Dough binge-eating when they were both supposed to be leading their team. But before he could answer, Jenny climbed into the canoe, buried her face in her hands, and started to wail.

"Uhhhh, are you OK?" Play Dough asked.

"Do I look OK?" Jenny snapped, lifting her face from her fingers. It was blotchy and red. Somehow, she still looked really pretty.

"You look sad, but—"

"My whole life is O-V-E-R, over."

Play Dough wondered why she'd come to the Boat Shack then. "Are you here for the canoe?" he asked. "Were you going to row out and then drown yourself in the lake?"

"WHAT?! NO!"

"Good. 'Cause that would suck."

"Why?" Jenny asked. "No one would miss me anyway."

"That's not true." *I would miss you.*

"Name one person."

"Jamie." *Me.*

"Jamie is bigger and better without me."

"Uh, OK. Your boyfriend then." Play Dough didn't want to say his stupid name aloud. Mostly because he was jealous of him, but also because "Christopher" was the name of conman Columbus. And news flash: He didn't find America. Amerigo Vespucci did.

"I don't have a boyfriend anymore!"

The news hit Play Dough like a ton of frozen pizzas. Did that mean Jenny was single? It had to mean she was single. Right?

Jenny took a piece of paper from the fold of her shorts and tore it up into a million pieces, all while making the sound of a killer whale: "AHWWWWAHHOOOOOOOW." It was spectacular. "Christoph. Er dumped meeee. In this. Letter," she said between sobs.

Say whaaaat? Christopher Columbus dumped *Jenny*? This dude had to be dumber than a single serving of potato chips. "Uh, why did he dump you?" he asked.

"Probab. Ly 'cause he's. Intimidated by. My beauty."

"Probably," Play Dough slipped. Panicking, he looked at the

shack's wall in search of a new conversation topic. "Nice wood," he blurted. He probably should have said, "Nice oars," or "Nice life vests," or "Nice fishing rods." But in that moment, Boat Shack vocab had escaped him.

Mid-sob, Jenny let out a laugh. "I can't believe you just said that."

"I'm into wood," Play Dough said, relieved he'd turned her frown upside down. "Wood walls, to be specific."

She laughed again. "I meant the part where you agreed that Christopher's intimidated by my beauty."

"Oh! I thought you meant *you're* intimidated by *my* beauty."

Jenny laughed even louder. "Stop making me laugh. I should be crying."

Exactly, Play Dough thought. He made her laugh. Christopher Columbus made her cry. Who was the catch here? Play Dough would never break up with Jenny in a letter. In fact, he would never break up with her PERIOD. "Do you want me to tape it back together?" he asked, picking up a few microscopic pieces of the letter. "Dover's got duct tape under his pillow."

"No thanks," Jenny said. "I never want to look at that letter again."

"Why not?" Play Dough asked. He loved hearing her trash-talk this guy. A little Kettle Corn on his lap and this would be the greatest *E! True Hollywood Story*, a show he sometimes watched with his sister, her dolls, and the cats.

"He actually congratulated me for being Lieutenant."

"What a moron," Play Dough scoffed. "You're not Lieutenant."

Jenny's face went rigid.

"Whoops. Sorry."

"It's fine. It's just—" She shook her head and her face relaxed a little. "I really, really wanted to be Lieutenant. And I thought Melman might be one. But not Jamie."

"I was surprised by that, too," Play Dough admitted. "No offense. I know she's your best friend."

"*Was* my best friend," Jenny said. "I lost her and my boyfriend and Lieutenant all in the past two days." She looked up at Play Dough with her wet blue eyes. "What did I do wrong?"

"Look," Play Dough said. "I've never met Christopher, but he sounds like a jerk." He waved his hand dramatically. "Good riddance! And Jamie? You didn't lose her. Color War can be intense, but it's over in less than a week. She's gonna be around until we're at least Junior Counselors, if not until we're playing Bingo in old-people homes with no teeth."

Jenny cringed. "Um, I will always have teeth."

Play Dough ate his lips to hide his whites. "Me ooh."

Jenny playfully shoved Play Dough, and the canoe rocked back and forth. They gripped the sides to steady themselves, giggling.

"And as far as Lieutenant goes," Play Dough began, "you and me—we would have made a good team." He took a breath, and then, nervous he'd said too much, plowed on. "Melman's cool, but I think if you were by my side, I might not be messing up so much."

Jenny burst with a little too much enthusiasm: "You're NOT messing up!"

Play Dough shot her a doubtful look.

"Fine." She sighed. "But honestly, it's not like you've done anything terrible. It's all been freak chance stuff. You just have to prove how awesome you are."

Play Dough bulged his eyes in horror. "How dare you use that word."

Jenny laughed. "Sorry, not 'awesome.' You just have to prove how 'psychedelic' you are. 'Cause you are. Psychedelic, I mean."

Play Dough really wished he had a proper definition of that word right now. Not knowing, all he could say was a lame "Thanks. Same, uh, to you."

Luckily, Jenny moved on. "So what exactly are *you* doing here?"

"Yeaaaaaaaaah." The truth was, Play Dough had started coming to the Boat Shack to eat in private when he was a Bunker Hill camper and his mom put him on a summer diet. He'd gained seven pounds. Of course, he didn't want to draw attention to his poundage around the best body in camp, so he tried to reframe his answer. "I got tired of screwing up. I came here to unwind."

Jenny looked down at Play Dough's feet, where a half-eaten loaf of white bread sat. "And eat carbohydrates?" Nothing got past her.

"When I rest, I get hungry." *Manners*, he thought. "Want some?"

"Isn't that for the fish?"

"There was leftover."

"Omigod, ew."

"Only some of it was in the lake."

Jenny chortled and rolled her eyes, which he found sexy,

because when she rolled them she also tilted her head back and her neck showed. Plus, he could see up her nose, and she had no boogers. Girls were amazing. Amendment: Jenny was amazing.

Jenny suddenly slapped her thighs. "LET'S MAKE A PLAN!"

"Uhhhhh." Play Dough was a little wary of Jenny and her plans since the last one brought about a raid war.

"What would you need to do to show you're the bestest Lieutenant?" she asked, her eye contact triggering yet another pool party in his pits.

Easy, he thought. "Find the Hatchet."

Jenny nodded to herself, plotting. "Yeah, I could help you with that. Since I'm not Lieutenant, I have a lot of free time to pick apart the clues." She laid her hands on Play Dough's shoulders. "And then, we'll find the Hatchet together! I'll get to do something Lieutenant-worthy, and you'll get to prove your amazing value to the team."

Play Dough grinned. There was no way Christopher appreciated Jenny like he did. Anyone with eyes could see she was beautiful, but Play Dough had a whole list of other reasons, *real reasons*, why she was so perfect-sauce. Jenny was passionate about plans and leadership, her giggles made him feel superhero tall, her crying was crazy like a whale's, and she had a good sense of humor even after a breakup. Maybe she did have what it took to be Lieutenant after all.

An accidental squeal over the PA interrupted Play Dough's internal love letter.

"So, are you down with the plan?" Jenny asked, stepping out of the canoe and offering her hand.

"Yeah," Play Dough said proudly, letting her pull him to his feet. "Just one thing. Maybe try to make up with Jamie?"

Jenny shrugged, confused. "Why do you care?"

Play Dough wasn't sure why he cared. He just thought it would make Jenny happy to have her best friend back. Friendship was the *F* in STARFISH, after all. He let his logic flow like poetry: "You're not bacon. You can't make everyone happy. But you can try. And I think, in turn, making up with Jamie will make you happy, too. But not as much as bacon."

"I don't eat bacon," Jenny confessed.

"Then you're a lost cause."

She giggled some more. "OK, fine! Whatever. I'll try."

Play Dough watched Jenny stuff the breakup confetti inside her pocket. He wasn't delusional—boyfriend or no boyfriend, he knew she'd never go out with a guy like him. But if this plan meant he could reclaim respect AND spend time with the girl of his dreams, then it was a win-win.

They walked out of the shack together, but Jenny turned toward the lake. "You coming?" Play Dough asked.

"You go ahead. I think I'll stay here for a few seconds on my own." She patted her pocket. "I'm gonna toss the pieces of this dumb letter into the lake."

"Cool."

"But thanks for cheering me up. And don't be so down about messing up. We have four more days to turn it all around."

Play Dough smiled. "Wars are won because of psychedelic leaders like us."

Playing Nice

Captain: Hello, Blue and White teams. Congrats on completing the second day of the war. Your Generals have some words of encouragement, and then TJ and I will announce the scores.

TJ: It's tied! Just kidding. It's not. But maybe. I don't know. I didn't look.

Captain: TJ.

TJ: First up, let's hear it for the Blue Psychedelic Sixties Generals!

General McCarville: Trippy dreams, our bell-bottomed Blues / Kick off those platforms and get in a snooze.

General Power: From sports to cheers to the Bucket Brigade / Keep it up, team, and we'll have it made!

TJ: Diggin' the rhymes, Blue. Next up, the White Awesome Eighties Generals!

General Ferrara: Sweatbands off and leg warmers down / We are the ones who run this town.

General Silver: Bucket Brigade's a minor loss / Tomorrow's Apache—we'll show Blue who's boss!

TJ: Oooooh!

Captain: I almost forgot to reveal the second Hatchet Hunt clue . . .

TJ: Dryer Sheets.

Captain: Great! And now for the scores! The following Sealed Envelopes have been assigned. Tug-o-War: White. Novelty Relays: White. Bucket Brigade: Blue.

TJ: And the sports 'n' spirits points so far . . . The anticipation . . . it's sucking your souls . . .

Captain: 256—Blue. 347—White.

TJ: OK, you warheads, nighty—

Jenny pulled her pink comforter up over her lap, flicked on her bed lamp, and looked out at her quiet cabin. Sophie was on her belly, reading a book about Woodstock. Slimey was listening to "Livin' on a Prayer" through leaky earphones while sketching scenery ideas for SING. On the porch, Jamie and Missi were squealing like dumb hyenas while "working" on White team rosters and Melman was politely asking them to zip it so she could concentrate on the rosters for Blue. Scottie, who was also on White, was out there saying stuff Jenny couldn't understand. Whenever Scottie got excited, she sounded like she had Pop Rocks in her mouth.

Jenny reached up into her cubby, knocked aside her standing ChapSticks, and grabbed a stack of letters from Christopher. Sometimes she liked to read through all five of them, admiring the way he chicken-scratched his letters, and asked deep questions about camp, and wrote sweet things that made her feel like a princess. But leafing through them now, her eyes stung with embarrassment. In some letters, he spelled "Jenny" with one *n*. The deepest question about camp was "How's kamp?" And the sweetest, most princess-y thing he'd ever written was "U r hott." Maybe Play Dough was right—Christopher was a jerk.

Even so, Jenny never imagined she'd get dumped, and that betrayal hurt. She flipped over one of Christopher's letters and wrote:

My heart cracked open, emoji in two,
Pining dumbly over the memories of you.
I'm feeling lost, so far from me,
I'll steal your credit card for a shopping spree.
BECAUSE YOU ARE THE WORST.

Jenny felt instantly better, even if just for a few seconds. At home, she wrote poetry a lot when Willamena made her feel like she didn't have what it took to be Second Most Popular. No one but Jenny's mom knew she wrote poetry. It was one of the uncool things about her that she'd shed, or in this case kept secret. Willamena would never let her stand by her side if she knew that Jenny preferred curling up with a pen and Moleskin notebook to long phone chats about who was the Most Popular in all of North Shore, Long Island.

Jenny looked down at her poem, and it kind of reminded her of bittersweet alma mater lyrics written for SING on the last night of Color War. Alma maters brought everyone together with rhyme schemes and heart-tugging imagery. Only, this poem was all bitter, no sweet. Like an anti-alma!

Now, thinking about almas, Jenny nostalgically tumbled into the memories of last summer's Blue Far Far Away SING songs, all from the *Shrek* soundtrack and featuring original lyrics written by last summer's Generals, Rick and Sara. First the march, to the tune of "Accidentally in Love." Next, the alma mater, to the tune of "Hallelujah." Then Jenny started to sing the White Land of Oz songs in her head. The march was to "If I Only Had a Brain" and the alma mater was to "Over the Rainbow." Even though Jenny and Jamie and Missi had been on Blue last summer, after the war, they'd learned the White songs, too. Their favorite lyrics covered the first verse of "Over the Rainbow": *"Sunsets over the rolling hills galore / Camp's a magical place where friendships grow and soar!"*

Wanting to share the nostalgia with her BFF now, Jenny looked through the window to the porch. Jamie and Missi were hand-clapping and laughing, excluding her to the max. Jenny swallowed last summer's SING memories, back to feeling hurt and neglected. *But hey*, she tried to assure herself, *this is normal*. Color War was always cutthroat the week leading up to SING. It wasn't until the winners were announced that everyone was reunited as one.

Jenny wondered if that was how Real War worked, but quickly decided that only in Color War did the opposing sides have preexisting superglued friendships that made forgiveness possible. Real War didn't have songs about Shrek and Dorothy, and dances to "Ease on Down the Road," and funny bits about Sara and Rick as Fiona and Shrek. And that was just so sad. Real soldiers could learn a thing or two from Rolling Hills.

Just then the cabin door swung open, and Jamie and Missi jumped inside, performing the swim-dance move. Their arms made long, unflattering shadows on the floor, and when they squatted with pinched noses, their shadows looked like Oompa Loompas. Jenny wanted to claw her eyes out. Forget patiently waiting for the war's end. Missi needed to be out of the picture STAT.

"Um, I'm reading," Sophie said.

For whatever reason, that made Missi collapse with laughter. Her bony elbows went into her sides, and she began sucking air in and out of the gap between her buckteeth.

"Omigod, wear your night retainer," Jenny snapped. "Normal people don't laugh like that. Also, we're all trying to concentrate on tasks for Color War."

"Sophie is. Slimey is," Missi said, twirling in a circle and pointing around the cabin. "But you're just"—she glanced at the papers on Jenny's lap—"reading letters from your boyfriend!"

"I know, but—"

Missi did the chicken. Jamie jumped on her back. They fell to the floor, laughing and saying "Ow" because there were jacks stabbing their butts.

Sophie ducked under her Halloween-themed comforter. Slimey upped the volume on her iPod. Jenny sat up, dumbstruck. How was it that her entire world had been turned upside down? What was next? Were brownies set to replace kale on the food pyramid? Was Miss Universe going to get thunder thigh implants? Was Melman the next Head Cheerleader? Was Jenny destined to be a garbage collector instead of a relationship therapist? What the what was going on?

She wanted to cry. It seemed like the natural thing to do in this sort of bizarre situation. Plus, it was probably the best way to get Jamie back on track. Right now they should be doing healing *I just got dumped* things like eating Ben & Jerry's Chocolate Therapy and making fun of Christopher's dumb summer haircut—a fauxhawk with his initials, CAZ, buzzed into the back of his head. All Jenny could do was hope Jamie noticed she was upset. That Jamie would put aside her anger and cuddle-spoon Jenny back to health. Together, they'd plot to find a new, hot, popular Christopher type who could complete Jenny's image.

Jenny started to think about sad stuff—abandoned baby deer, lipstick testing on sloths, Caesar salads with anchovies—but they weren't doing the trick. She let herself fall into hurtful memories, like when she and Willamena weighed themselves side by side, and Willamena bragged about being 5.6 pounds lighter than her. And the Snapchats that went out about how, compared to Willamena, Jenny was a hotless tamale. And the time that Willamena pulled a *Mean Girls* and wouldn't let Jenny sit at her lunch table because she was wearing baby pink, not neon pink as they'd discussed the month before. Now her eyes felt prickly. *One last step.* She popped her lids open, stared at her bed lamp, and let her tear ducts work their magic. She blinked, and two tears flew down her face. *Success!*

No one seemed to notice. The problem, she guessed: It was

dark. So she sniffled. No response. She coughed. Nothing. She whimpered. Nada. The bigger problem, she realized: It was loud. Missi's and Jamie's giggles were bouncing off the cabin walls, drowning her out. She'd have to ditch subtlety. "JAMIE!!!" she screamed.

The giggling stopped. Jamie craned her neck up at Jenny. "Ummmm, yeah?"

"I'm crying," Jenny told her.

"OK." Jamie smirked at Missi. Missi smirked back.

"It's about Christopher."

"Omigod," Jamie said in a way that sounded familiar, but not nasal like how she normally spoke. "Do you miss him?"

Jenny slipped into a montage of Christopher memories. (1) The time they danced at the Disney Club for teens. They'd stayed out till midnight, reenacting the famous *Titanic* pose at the bow of the cruise ship. (2) The time they texted for an hour exclusively using emojis. *What was the meaning of mustache, turban, kimono, angel, mountain bike, pumpkin?!?* she'd wondered. Nothing, she'd learned—she'd been texting with Christopher's dog, Felix! (3) The time they shared their fifth kiss at the movies watching . . . something? Jenny couldn't remember because they'd been so busy making out!

"Hello, Jenny? Are you having a brain cramp?"

Jenny snapped back to Jamie, who was standing there with her little hands on her little hips. "Oh. No, about the cramp," Jenny said. "Yes, about Christopher. I do miss him."

Jamie shook her head, baffled. "I was making fun of you when I asked that. I don't care if you miss Christopher."

That's when Jenny realized why Jamie had sounded familiar. She'd been imitating her. Jenny felt her heart crack, like the emoji in her poem. "Why don't you care?"

"Are you seriously asking me that?"

Missi stood, swatted a jack from her butt, and threw her lanky arm around Jamie's shoulders. "After what you said to Jamie yesterday, she doesn't want to hear anything but an apology."

"I just said I'm sorry."

"No you didn't," Jamie said. "You fake-cried and said you miss Christopher."

Jenny should have known Jamie would pick up on the light-staring trick. Did Jamie know Jenny better than Jenny knew herself? Now Jenny wanted to cuddle-spoon with Jamie even more. "Well, I meant to say it. I'm sorry, OK?"

"Are you *actually* sorry?" Jamie asked.

"Um, yeah, are you deaf? GOD." Silence. Even the crickets stopped chirping. "Why are you being mean to me?" Jenny bit her tongue to keep her face from contorting into real, ugly crying. "You're not embarrassing yourself, OK? You're doing a good job. Now are you happy?"

"That's not the only reason why I'm mad at you," Jamie said.

"Why else are you mad at me?"

Jamie shrugged.

"Is it because I was mad at you first?" Jenny asked. "I have a right to be mad at you."

"So you *are* mad at me for getting Lieutenant?" Jamie asked.

"No," Jenny lied.

"So you're a liar."

"What?! No. I don't know!"

"You don't know if you're a liar?"

Jenny scream-grunted, threw off her comforter, and bounced to her knees. "I should have been Lieutenant, and you know it! As my best friend, you should have made me feel better!"

"As *my* best friend you should have supported me," Jamie said. "The world doesn't revolve around you."

"The sun's first name isn't Jenny," Missi interjected.

"SHUT UP, MISSI!" Jenny yelled.

"Hey," Scottie called, hustling into Faith Hill Cabin. Melman trailed behind her. "What in the bloody ham is going on?" Jenny, Jamie, and Missi went quiet. "C'mon, no Color War in the cabin. We are on neutral grounds here, oi. Can we settle?"

Jenny chewed on her lip, thinking about how Willamena dealt with hierarchy rebellions. Anytime Jenny spent too much time with Riley, for example, Willamena would put Jenny down and give Riley the silent treatment. Other times, she pretended to be obsessed with Riley, and told Jenny she should just make new friends. That was the way Popular girls stayed Popular. So, no, Jenny would not settle quietly while Jamie and Missi walked all over her. She dished Jamie the final argument: "Lieutenant Nederbauer is a mistake. A joke. Everyone's thinking it, and I'm the only one brave enough to say it."

"Oh, I think you've made that super-clear," Jamie said. She took Missi's hand. "Let's go, Twenty-seven."

"Yes, please, Lieutenant Twenty," Missi answered. "Leave Fifty to her fakeness."

Jenny scrunched her eyes in confusion. Why were they speaking in numbers? Was it a White team thing? An Eighties thing? Why had they called her "Fifty"? Did she have early onset wrinkles or something? Maybe now that she was so close to real, ugly tears?

Jamie pulled Missi into the bathroom, whispering. Words like "selfish" and "bully" and "conceited" floated to Jenny's ears. She had the urge to scream: "STOP IT! DON'T YOU GET IT? CHRISTOPHER DUMPED ME!" But surely Missi and Jamie would think she was lying to get attention. Or, even worse, they would laugh and tell her that she deserved heartbreak. That she deserved to be single and lonely and obese from Ben & Jerry's Chocolate Therapy.

Jenny shoved Christopher's letters back into her cubby and slipped into the same montage of memories. But now she saw their relationship for what it truly was: pathetic. (1) Jenny had tricked Christopher into doing the *Titanic* pose for Instagram likes. (2) The emoji-texting with Felix was actually pretty humiliating. (3) When they made out, Christopher used too much tongue, like he was giving her a tooth cleaning. Jenny hadn't told a soul. Because what would her followers do? Unfollow her, that's what.

Except for Play Dough. He was the kind of guy who'd follow her to the moon and back. He hadn't judged Jenny for getting dumped. And soggy lake bread was no Chocolate Therapy, but still, it was food, and he'd offered it to her to make her feel better.

Jenny suddenly felt moved to help Play Dough just as she'd

promised. What would she do if she lost him, too? She wouldn't pull a Melman and chop off all her hair, or drown herself in the lake, but she'd probably text her mom, demanding that she be picked up early like some friendless loser. To ensure that it wouldn't come to that, Jenny stuck her earplugs in to block out Missi and Jamie's mean whisper-giggling, snuck her diary out from inside her pillowcase, and began to decipher today's Hatchet Hunt clues.

Clue 1: Lady and the Tramp
- Lady and the Tramp is a movie, so maybe it's in the office, where they store old movies. But that's a private space, so no.
- Lady rhymes with . . . ? Oh! Shady!
- Tramp rhymes with: camp, damp, lamp, ramp, stamp
- Hiding spots: somewhere in camp, somewhere damp, inside a lamp, by the ramp (is there a ramp?!), in a mailbox, somewhere shady

Clue 2: Dryer Sheets
- Laundry—like, inside one of the machines?
- Rhymes with: higher cleats—so, soccer?!

- Dryer Sheets scrambled is: She Steer Dry—so a dry canoe?
- Is it just inside a dryer sheets box or is that too obvious?

Jenny crossed the whole page out and squeezed her eyes shut in frustration. These clues were hard. Even with time on her side, she didn't have a brain for puzzles. Whenever her dad did the Sunday *New York Times* crossword, he'd ask her the five easiest questions. And never once did she get any of them right. "That's OK, Jennifer," he'd say. "Show me your endangered polar bear PowerPoint again. Very impressive!" But she wasn't impressive. And she needed to be in order to find the Hatchet.

Jenny decided to think positively like Slimey might, or even Melman. *My diary!* She flipped through to find Hatchet Hunt inspiration. And that's when she stumbled upon something weird. Her "Faith Hillers—Strengths and Weaknesses" page was unfolded. Had she left it that way by accident? No way. Which meant—*OMIGOD*—someone had snooped! But who knew about Jenny's diary? Maybe Jamie. Who knew where she kept it? No one. *But . . . Wait a second . . . OMIGODOMIGOD.*

TOTAL SCORES	50/50	20/50	27/50	30/50	35/50	36/50

The final tallies of Jenny's chart jumped off the page. Jamie was worth twenty points. Missi was worth twenty-seven. Jenny was worth fifty. *That's what those numbers meant!* Jenny's mind flashed to the night before Color War. *Nosybody Missi* had caught her writing in her diary. She'd shone her flashlight onto it. She'd watched Jenny put it away!

Ugh, Jenny thought, feeling mad and guilty all at once. Maybe she could explain herself to them. She could say something like "I didn't mean to rank you, I swear." But then they might ask, "If you didn't mean it, then why did you do it?" And Jenny didn't have an answer to that question. She frantically yanked out her earplugs. From the bathroom, Jamie and Missi's trash talk pierced her ears.

Missi: "Omigod, wouldn't camp be so much better if Jenny hadn't crashed the party four summers ago? Remember how close we all were in One Tree Hill Cabin, and how everything got so cliquey as soon as she came for our Two Tree Hill summer?"

Jamie: "That's so weird to think about. We'd all be best friends still and have no drama!"

Missi: "Drama-free is the way to be! Go Miss-Jam!"

Jenny felt a stabbing pain in her chest. Had Missi and Jamie seriously come up with a mash-up name for themselves? Did they honestly wish she'd never come to Rolling Hills at all? Her mind flooded with memories of her very first summer at camp. She'd been so nervous coming into a cabin where the social ladder was already in place. But when she'd gotten there, she was shocked to find that "Popular Girl" was up for grabs and no one was grabbing! Naturally, she'd grabbed it. It wasn't her fault that Jamie followed her around like an untrained puppy. Or that Missi then followed her and Jamie around like some hyper farm cat. It wasn't her fault that Melman and Slimey began to stick together like almond butter and jelly. Or that Sophie retreated into even weirder weirdness. Nothing was Jenny's fault. When new kids came to camp, things changed.

"Are you Hatchet Hunting tomorrow morning?" Missi asked Jamie.

"I can't," Jamie said. "The officers have a SING meeting."

"Cool. Then I'll just wait to hunt with you at Rest Hour."

And then the dynamic duo strolled out of the bathroom, arm in arm, past Jenny's top bunk. They paused, eyed Jenny's diary, and smirked at each other.

"Is that your diary?" Missi asked.

"That's none of your business," Jenny responded.

"Were you just writing about us?" Missi asked.

"Not everything is the Jamie and Missi Show," Jenny said.

"We go by 'Miss-Jam,'" Missi said proudly. "I don't know if you've heard."

"I haven't," Jenny lied. "But wow, that's such a creative name."

Miss-Jam nodded.

"If you weren't writing about us behind our backs," Missi asked, "then what were you writing about?"

"The Hatchet Hunt," Jenny answered.

Missi and Jamie looked at her, puzzled. "Why?" Jamie asked. "You've always said you're bad at clues and hunts and stuff."

"Yeah," Missi agreed. "Did you forget that last summer Play Dough hid a rotting fish in your cubby, and you couldn't even find it?"

"Neither could you," Jenny snapped. "And I'm not bad at

clues and hunts and stuff anymore. I know exactly where the Hatchet is. And I'm going to find it with Lieutenant Play Dough, who believes I'm a Hatchet prodigy."

"He said that?" Jamie asked.

"Obviously," Jenny said. "Tomorrow I'm going to make camp *her*story. No one's going to remember the mini-Lieutenant who unfroze her T-shirt." She glared at Missi. "Or her lame follower friend. They'll remember me."

Miss-Jam gasped in shock. But then, because they had the luxury of each other to lean on, they laughed it off. "I can't believe you just said that!" Jamie squealed.

Missi joined in: "The day you make camp *her*story will be the day I—!"

Jenny plugged her ears and curled up in a fetal position facing the wall. *What the what have I done?!?* She didn't know where the Hatchet was! Sure, it could be in a mailbox or in a dryer sheets box or somewhere shady, but she could search those places for days and still not find it.

She went to slip her diary inside her pillowcase. But then she hesitated. She needed a new hiding spot. If she stuck her diary back inside her pillowcase, then Jamie and Missi would find her pathetic Hatchet Hunt brainstorm.

And then an idea hit her so hard, the plugs nearly popped from her ears. What if she could create a new brainstorm—one that didn't seem pathetic at all? What if she could lead Missi and Jamie to a Fake Hatchet in a forbidden hiding spot, costing the White team the Sealed Envelope? And Play Dough could help. She tapped her pen against her chin in thought. Where was off-limits other than past hiding spots and toilets? *Hmmm.* She tapped harder. *Hmmmmmm.* PRIVATE SPACES!

Jenny brainstormed private spaces, but all the ones she could think of were inside cabins. Jamie and Missi knew better than to fall for a Fake Hatchet in an obviously forbidden domain. *Hmmmm. What if . . .* It hit her. Insanely hard. THE CAPTAIN'S GOLF CART! Jenny's mind flashed back to three Color Wars ago when she'd shadowed Lieutenant Acosta, who'd bet the Hatchet was hidden inside there. All the officers debated whether that was a "Private Space." Technically, it lived outdoors and was used by a lot of other staff for camp tours. And it was no more private than a toilet, where the Hatchet had been hidden before. So they'd asked the Captain if her cart was off-limits. Her response: "Absolutely." But Jenny had never shared that story with Jamie or Missi.

Jenny smiled to herself, opened her diary, thought hard about the clues, and scribbled:

Clue 1: Lady and the Tramp
- Who is the "Lady" in charge of camp? Answer: THE CAPTAIN.
- What is something she has that could trample stuff? Answer: HER GOLF CART.

Clue 2: Dryer Sheets

- Who uses dryer sheets so that her staff shirts come out pressed and fresh? Answer: THE CAPTAIN.
- How does she get her laundry to the laundry room? Answer: HER GOLF CART.

Jenny folded the page over and wrote *TOP SECRET: HATCHET HUNT* on the flap. She waited until Missi had an eye on her, and then, pretending to be stealthy, she shoved her diary in a new hiding spot—under her mattress. Then she set a two-hour timer on her pink sports watch and tried, tried, tried to quiet her excitement for a couple hours of shut-eye.

Jenny's eyes popped open a minute before the timer was supposed to go off, which she took to be a sign that her plan, however risky, was exactly right. She threw on black leggings and a black hoodie, climbed down her bunk ladder, and tiptoed past Miss-Jam cuddle-spooning. She gathered a towel, Melman's blue hairspray, Missi's white hairspray, Sophie's flashlight, and Slimey's colored pencils. She shoved it all in Jamie's backpack. Then she snuck out the front door.

Jenny climbed up and down three hills, hopping into as many shadows as she could. It was a pretty night—the stars were glistening like diamonds. The wind whipped her cheeks, and drowned out the crickets, and made the fallen leaves rustle into mini-cyclones. As Jenny approached the forest, part of her wondered if this plan was insane. Sneaking out? In the middle of the night? Into the woods? Yes, it was absolutely nuts. *But sometimes crazy is the only way*, she reminded herself.

She put her hood up and tied the drawstrings into a bow beneath her chin. Then, feeling a bit warmer and more secure, she began the last leg of her trek. She dodged a skunk, a chipmunk, a plastic bag she thought was a bat, and then a real bat before she reached her first destination: the Tool Shed. She'd survived! This was it! Hoorah! She went to push the door open but it was chain locked. *Nooooooooo!* Great for safety, disastrous for her plan.

Jenny did a lap around the shed, desperately searching for a way to break in. She rounded the last corner and, Holy Bingo! At ground level, a rotting piece of the wall had been gnawed away at (presumably by a feral opossum), leaving a jagged hole. Jenny felt the wood—it was damp and nasty. She prayed that (a) she'd be skinny enough to squeeze through without getting splintered to death, and (b) she wouldn't get attacked by any opossums in the process.

Jenny took a deep *Am I really doing this?* breath in. She exhaled, thinking, *Yes, girl, you are.* She climbed through the hole, arms first, then her head, then her torso, and then she wiggled her hips to fit the rest of her body inside. She collapsed onto a muddy floor littered with sawdust. *Victory!*

Her heart slamming, Jenny flicked on her flashlight and shone it around. Lots of cobwebs, lots of tools: gardening hoes, rakes, brooms, saws, drills, hammers, and . . . YES, A HATCHET! She pulled a creaky stepladder out from the corner, climbed up four rungs, and pulled it from the wall. It was heavy and a little rusty and was absolutely perfect for her con.

Covered in sawdust, wood, and probably opossum poop, Jenny crawled out of the shed and unpacked her supplies. She sprayed the Hatchet blue and white and penciled COLOR WAR on the handle. She wrapped it in the towel, slunk out of the forest, and crept ten paces to the side of Hill Hall where the Captain's golf cart was parked. *Where should I . . . ?* She knew she couldn't leave the Hatchet in an obvious spot, like on the seat or in the back basket. But there was no glove compartment, or any other compartments for that matter. *Maybe it will fit in the . . .* She lifted the white cushion seat and slid the Hatchet underneath. It fit, totally lump-free.

And then, overridden by *Wow! Omigod! Plans be planning!* exhilaration, Jenny shadow-hopped back to Faith Hill Cabin, changed out of her black clothes, returned her cabinmates' supplies, and promptly fell asleep for six satisfying hours.

August 14th

Dear Grandma,

Got your present. Got your white hat and white bandana and white hairspray. Thanks a lot! Tell Grandpa that my head is officially whiter than his was before the funny dye job.

This week has been the greatest week of my life. Remember Jamie? She's the really cute one who looks like a Gap Kids model. She's my Best Friend.

Missi is the best BFF and sidekick. Kick powwwww! Hahaha—how r the cats and cows?

Jamie wrote that! She's so silly sometimes. Big kitty cat kisses to Happy, Sleepy, Grumpy, Dopey, Bashful, Doc, and Snow WHITE!!! Go White!

Love,
Missi + Miss-Jam

Hacked Hunt

"All right, guys, almost at Hill Hall," Play Dough called over his shoulder to Dover and Smelly. They weren't moving like snails or anything, Play Dough was just hustling hard.

"Dude-a-cris, why are you walking like a penguin?" Dover asked.

"I'm speed walking," Play Dough said. "My mom taught me."

Dover tried, but he kept his knees locked, so it looked like he was on stilts. Smelly doubled over with laughter. Then Dover stilt-walked to the closest tree and started to climb.

Play Dough went to check his watch, but he realized that he'd lost it in the lake two summers ago. "Dover, what are you doing?"

"Hatchet Hunting, man. Monkey-style."

Play Dough slapped his forehead. "No, c'mon, we're gonna be late. The Hatchet is by Hill Hall."

"Who says?" Dover asked.

"Jenny."

That's when Smelly officially stopped laughing and Dover dropped down from the tree. "What's Jenny got to do with the Hatchet?" Dover asked suspiciously.

"I just said. She knows where it is."

"If Jenny knows where it is, then why doesn't she get it herself?" Smelly asked. "Is it in a hard-to-reach spot or something?"

"I dunno," Play Dough said. "Probably." He didn't want to tell the guys about the arrangement he and Jenny had made in the Boat Shack. They might think that he doubted their hunting skills, or that he was falling so hard for Jenny that he'd do just about anything she said.

"Are you sure you're not just getting mixed up in another plan of hers?" Dover asked.

"I'm sure," Play Dough said. "Jenny's changed. She doesn't make bad plans anymore." He didn't know why he'd said that. He guessed, deep down, he hoped it was true.

"I don't think the Hatchet's by Hill Hall," Dover said. "*Lady and the Tramp* is about dogs. Dogs are better than cats. Cats purr. When Claudia Cooking makes one-eyed sailors—also known as eggs in a basket—she always says, 'Oooh! *Purr*-fect.' And dryer sheets? Claudia uses *baking sheets* that *dry* after she washes them. As far as the newest clue—'Toil and Trouble'—Claudia is a twin, just like Mary-Kate and Ashley are twins and stars of the 1993 hit movie *Double, Double, Toil and Trouble*."

"So?" Play Dough asked.

"So it's near the Cooking Shack."

Play Dough checked his watchless wrist again like a moron.

"Back me up, Smelly," Dover said.

"Oh, I don't know," said Smelly.

"You're the one who FOUND OUR UNDERWEAR last summer. Do you think I'm right—that the Hatchet's by the Cooking Shack?"

"Uh, could be."

"See?" Dover said, grinning at Play Dough. "It could be."

"You know that Slimey led me to the underwear, right?" Smelly asked. "I'm not an expert finder of stuff."

Dover just winked.

Play Dough groaned. "Look, Jenny said to meet at the very beginning of Rest Hour, so I'm headed to Hill Hall."

"General Power said something was up with you," Dover said.

"He said that?" Play Dough asked.

Dover shrugged. Smelly picked at a scab on his elbow, clearly uncomfortable.

"Guys. Tell me now. What did General Power say?"

Dover sighed. "That he didn't know what TJ and the Captain were thinking when they picked you."

Play Dough tried to stand tall, but his bones felt like they were crumbling. "What did you say back to him? Did you tell him all the good stuff about me? Explain why I'm Lieutenant material?"

"Uhhhhhhh," Dover said.

Play Dough looked at Smelly. "Smellsky?"

"We almost said that stuff," Smelly said.

"What did you say instead?" Play Dough asked.

"We said nothing," admitted Smelly.

"You guys let him say that about me?" Play Dough asked.

"Dover, I've known you almost half my life. You didn't defend me?"

"Dude, Ashanti Power is our General. Plus, he's the real deal. When he was a cadet, he ran three miles through the woods with a forty-four-pound backpack on while carrying a stretcher and WON NATIONALS."

"So?" Play Dough wasn't sure what that had to do with Color War.

"He's every Eagle Scout's idol," Dover said. "Plus, you *have* been messing up a lot."

Play Dough could hardly believe it. Sure, General Power was impressive when it came to Real War stuff. It made sense that a JROTC stud would think Lieutenant Play Dough was a clown. But his *own best friends* thought he was failing the team? Didn't they know Color War had a different vibe? "Look, if you want to come with me, groovy-sauce. If you want to search the Cooking Shack, go bananas." Play Dough speed-walked away, and somehow that inspired them to follow suit.

It was a sunny and stuffy afternoon, and Play Dough arrived at Hill Hall, the big house where all the Upper Staffers lived, with angry creases of sweat in his T-shirt. He tried to hide them by crossing his arms over his chest, but that just exposed his monster pit stains. He dropped his arms to his sides. Then he spotted Jenny standing in front of an oak tree, waving him over. Just walking toward her made his hurt level slide down a notch. "Hey, Jenny. What's going on?"

She lifted her big round sunglasses up to her forehead and

squinted over Play Dough's shoulder. "What are *they* doing here?" she hissed.

Play Dough looked back at Smelly and Dover, both stilt-walking now. "Oh, those guys?" He itched to say, "They don't trust us. I'm unworthy of being Lieutenant and you're a conniving planner." Instead he said, "They came to help. Don't worry, they're on Blue like us." Then he wanted to pinch himself. Of course Jenny knew who her teammates were. Even if she'd forgotten, Smelly and Dover were dressed bluer than blueberries.

Smelly dropped the stilt-walking and normal-walked the rest of the way to the tree. "Hi, Jenny," he said nervously. He hadn't talked to her since the Egg Toss, and the trauma of her yelling at him seemed to rush back—his cheeks got red and he averted his eyes to Dover, who'd fully committed to stilt-walking until he touched the tree bark.

"Waz up?" Dover asked Jenny. "We're here to do the hard reaching."

"Ew," Jenny said. She glared at Play Dough. "Make this problem go away."

Play Dough gave her a thumbs-up, pretending he understood what the problem was. It was time to delegate. "You on the problem, Dov?"

"On it, Lieutenant!" He clapped his feet together, waiting to be told what to do next.

Jenny's sky-blue eyes turned dark denim. "You, Dover. You, Smelly. Are. The. Problem." She paused. "No offense."

Smelly shook his head politely. Dover cocked his chin, confused. Play Dough lowered his head, embarrassed. If the guys already doubted him and Jenny, he wasn't sure excluding them would make things better. "Jenny, are you sure they can't—?"

"Positive," Jenny broke in. "It's all part of the— It'll complicate things if— OK, here's why: You and I deserve the credit. Split four ways, no one will remember my involvement, and General Power will hardly be impressed with you."

"Yeah, but the points all go to the same place," Dover said.

"General Power said it's a Blue effort," Smelly added. "Are we in competition with each other?"

"Omigod, go away. Byeeeee." She hooked her arm through Play Dough's arm and led him toward the side of Hill Hall.

Play Dough mouthed "Sorry" over his shoulder at Dover and Smelly, who were standing there, baffled. "You're picking *her* over *us*?" Dover called after him. "No soldier left behind! We're your bros, PD! Bros before hatchets!"

Before Play Dough could assure his bros that they ranked above hatchets, Jenny yanked him face-forward. "Just ignore them. They'll get over it."

"Uh, I don't know." A part of Play Dough felt justified—if the guys didn't defend him to General Power, why should he defend them to Jenny? But Play Dough had enough at stake. And petty revenge didn't seem to be the answer. Plus, what if Dover was right and the Hatchet really was hidden in the Cooking Shack? He'd kick himself for ditching them to follow Jenny's lead. *Wait*, he stumbled. *Did* Jenny even have a lead? How was she so sure the Hatchet was by Hill Hall?

Play Dough tried to recall his lunchtime conversation with

her by the salad bar. She'd spooned tuna onto his plate and whispered: "The Hatchet. Hill Hall. Rest Hour. We will be heroes." Then she'd touched his hand to her heart and said, "I have a premonition." But Play Dough hadn't been thinking straight with tuna on his plate and his hand so close to Jenny's boob, and also, he'd never heard the word "premonition" before. For all he knew, Jenny was using big vocab to tell him that she had gas pains in her chest.

Now she asked sweetly, "Do you believe me that I know where it is?"

Does she read minds? Play Dough wondered. She must, so he decided to be totally honest. "I believe that you *think* you know where it is."

She giggled and playfully smacked his gut, which was especially uncomfortable fifteen minutes after a double grilled cheese. Play Dough swallowed a burp.

"You're funny," she said. "I told you I'd keep my promise, so I will. I will lead you to the Hatchet."

"What about Jamie?" Play Dough asked. "How'd making up with her go?"

"Omigod, we talked and she was mad at me for deeper reasons, but now I know what they are, so, like, I have a better idea how to handle things."

Play Dough didn't fully understand what that meant, but he'd known Jenny and Jamie long enough to know that there was no point in trying to understand the ins and outs of their friendship. He was just glad they were able to hash stuff out. "Cool. So where should we start looking?"

"Um, let's see . . . " Jenny rounded the corner of Hill Hall where special visitors usually parked and then gasped to a halt. "Don't be obvious about it, but"—she cupped her hands around Play Dough's ear and whispered—"someone is trespassing on the Captain's golf cart." Her breath tickled him down to his toes.

Respecting Jenny's request for subtlety, Play Dough pretended to look at the tree behind the golf cart but really just looked at the golf cart. It was parked on the grass by the side of Hill Hall, and a girl was half visible behind it, rummaging through the sports equipment in the back basket. "Is she looking for the Hatchet?" Play Dough whispered in Jenny's ear. He wondered if his breath had the same effect on her, especially now that she was freshly single.

Jenny shrugged. "I think so. Should we tell her that the golf cart's off-limits so that she doesn't get in trouble? She might not know."

"Uhhhh." It was in Play Dough's nature to help people, but the trespasser was decked in White. As much as he wanted to do the right thing, he was a little confused as to what the right thing was. Should he betray Blue to warn White? Or let the girl get her team in trouble so that he and Jenny had a better chance of finding the Hatchet themselves?

"Um," Jenny said. "That's Jamie."

Play Dough took a step forward and squinted through the sun. Yup, that was Jamie's head emerging from a pile of kickballs.

"We have to warn her," Jenny said. She touched Play Dough's

biceps, which was the part of his body he was most proud of—sometimes his bulk passed for muscle. "It'll mean more coming from you, PD, since you're both Lieutenants."

"Are you sure you want me to—?"

Jenny nodded.

Play Dough smiled to himself. He was right about Jenny—her deranged plans were a thing of the past. She could so easily just walk away and let Jamie and her team suffer the consequences, but no. She was choosing to save her best friend from disaster. And it was clear to Play Dough that the right thing to do was to help. "Uhhh, Jamie?"

Jamie froze and then darted her head up, a gerbil in headlights. "What do you want?" she asked.

"The Hatchet's not in there."

"I'm not stupid."

Play Dough looked at Jenny for help, but Jenny gave him nothing. "OK, we just—"

"You can pretend to look out for me all you want," Jamie cut in. "You both know I'm right."

Just then, Missi rolled out from under the golf cart, flat on her back, on a skateboard. "It's here."

"WHAT?!" Jamie screamed. "YOU FOUND IT?!!?"

Play Dough found himself stumbling forward with envy.

"No, not yet," Missi said. "I was agreeing with you. That the Hatchet is hidden here." Then she rolled back under the cart.

Play Dough stepped back to Jenny's side and whispered: "What if they *are* right? What if the cart's *not* off-limits?"

"Impossible," Jenny assured him. "Let's just go."

Play Dough watched Missi and Jamie scurry in and around the golf cart. What did they know that he didn't? What if the Hatchet really was in there, and here he was, letting it go without a fight? Then what kind of Lieutenant would he be? A pushover. A traitor. An embarrassment to his team and his friends and family.

"Apparently Jamie's still upset with me," Jenny sulked. "I wish she understood that friendship is more important than war, just like you said. You know?"

Play Dough watched Missi scour the tires and Jamie toy with the wheel. "Uh-huh," he said absentmindedly, imagining the Hatchet appearing from some secret compartment. If he could just swoop in and grab it, oh boy, would things turn around for him! He could see it now: General Power would exclaim, "Holy turds! Lieutenant Play Dough isn't hopeless after all!" And Play Dough would crowd-surf his team, like he'd seen teenagers do at concerts on YouTube. Plus, his family would freak out with pride—at Thanksgiving, they'd honor him with a plateful of turkey drumsticks drenched in gravy.

"Let's go, Play Dough," Jenny said, tugging at his sleeve.

Play Dough didn't budge. He couldn't peel his eyes off the golf cart.

"I mean it," Jenny insisted. She looked nervous. "If Jamie wants to be mean about it, then let's just leave her alone."

Play Dough's heart was pumping like mad. He clenched and unclenched his fists, trying to restrain himself. But what was the point of holding back? Jamie and Missi were being awful-sauce friends. Jenny was trying to protect Jamie, and this was how Jamie treated her? Jamie and Missi didn't deserve to find the Hatchet. Play Dough did. He'd do it for Jenny, for himself, for his family, for Blue. "I have to do it," he said. Jenny looked at him funny. "I HAVE TO!"

"Do what?!" Jenny asked, her eyes flashing with panic.

Play Dough didn't have time to respond. He was already racing toward the golf cart. Missi and Jamie scrambled to block him, but Play Dough was an unblockable force (to skinny girls). He belly flopped onto the front seat. Something underneath the cushion dug into his chest. He hoped it was the Hatchet, but not the blade, though his adrenaline was pumping so hard he wasn't sure he cared either way. Bring on the blood!

"Leave it, Play Dough! We're going to get in big trouble!" Jenny cried. "Seriously!"

He understood that Jenny didn't want him to get in trouble, but he wouldn't get in trouble if the Hatchet was, in fact, underneath him. He clawed under the cushion and felt—*phew*, no blade—a wooden handle! Missi and Jamie were screaming bloody murder now. He pulled the handle out and—thank you, War Lord—THE HATCHET HAD BEEN FOUND!!!

Play Dough launched himself from the golf cart, tore the protective towel from the Hatchet's blade, and held it high. It was beautifully tagged with blue and white graffiti and looked sharper than cheddar. "I got it for you, Jenny! I got it!" She was hiding behind a tree. "I got it!" he cried again, hoping to shake her from her fear of trouble. She peeked out, her eyes darting.

A deafening whistle sounded. The Captain kicked open the side door of Hill Hall. "What is going on?!"

Jamie and Missi looked down at their feet. Play Dough got why they were bummed—they hadn't found the Hatchet—but Jenny? Why wasn't she bursting with excitement like he was? Was she mad at him? Nervous that Missi and Jamie were mad at her? Well, she didn't have to worry! He and Jenny were heroes. She'd followed through with her promise, and now so would he.

Play Dough walked to the Captain, knelt down, and placed the Hatchet at her feet. "Jenny and I found the Hatchet, your highness judge. The Sealed Envelope goes to Blue."

The Captain bent down and picked up the Hatchet. She examined it, perplexed. "This isn't the Color War Hatchet. This is Eddie Duskin's."

"Who?" Play Dough asked.

"The groundskeeper." She flipped it over and showed him the bottom of the handle where e.d. was engraved. Play Dough's heart bobbed with confusion. "Where'd you find it?" the Captain demanded.

Play Dough looked back at the Captain's golf cart with dread. It was a mess—the cushion was down by the pedals, there were muddy handprints on the sides, and the sports equipment from the back was strewn all over the ground.

"My golf cart is private, Brian," she said. He took note: No "Lieutenant." No "Play Dough." Just "Brian." The Captain was full-blown shaming him. "Do any of you care to explain?" she asked, her pressing stare hopping from camper to camper. "Brian?" she prompted.

Play Dough wanted to shield Blue from trouble, but the imposter Hatchet was as much a mystery to him as it was to the Captain. "Uh, I dunno."

"Jamie?" she asked.

Jamie started to shake. "I—I—I didn't do it!" she cried.

Play Dough felt a pang of guilt. He wanted to comfort her like how he comforted his little sister—with a giant bear hug—but he and Jamie didn't have that kind of relationship.

Luckily, Missi hugged Jamie so he didn't have to. "It's OK, Jamie, you can tell the Captain what happened."

Jamie sniffled into Missi's shoulder. "Jenny's over there, hiding behind that tree. And she told us it was—"

"I DIDN'T *TELL YOU* ANYTHING!" Jenny stepped out to scream.

"Jenny, get over here," the Captain said irritably. Jenny sulked over. "Go on, Jamie."

"She *wrote* it," Missi clarified. "Jenny wrote that the Hatchet was in your golf cart, so we went to find it. And then Play Dough rushed to find it, too, and he won."

"Well, to be clear, nobody won anything," the Captain said. "Points will be deducted. Penalties will be implemented." Play Dough groaned. Jamie and Missi whimpered. Jenny was still. "Jenny, did you take Eddie's Hatchet?"

"Play Dough wasn't supposed to go after it. Just Jamie and Missi."

“That’s not what I asked you.”

“I wrote it in my diary. Jamie and Missi snooped!”

“Again, not the question.”

Jenny pursed her lips together and committed to silence and zero eye contact.

Play Dough’s mind drowned with questions. What had Jenny done? Had she just used him for another one of her plans? Had she ever intended to find the Hatchet with him? Or was she just trying to make him look like the world’s biggest hack?

August 14

Dear Mom and Dad,

Color War has been a mad dash of activity. But after an incident of Blue brotherhood betrayal, we took the time to connect with a Rolling Hills staff member: Claudia Cooking. Claudia Cooking's real name is Claudia Karla Roberta Rojas. It's just that if you're a counselor with a specialty, that specialty becomes your camp last name. She is from Costa Rica. Her favorite food to make is ceviche. Here, she learned to bake challah. She is 63 years old and plans on returning to Rolling Hills until she is 103. The Hatchet is not in the Cooking Shack.

Ben

August 14

Dear Dad,

A big yip-yip-yip from the Blue team!

This afternoon was the Apache Relay. It's this epic relay race with 200 events like pogo-sticking, swimming laps in pajamas, washing your hair in the lake, and reciting the al-phabet backward. I had to run the bases as fast as possible against Lieutenant Totle, and we were neck and neck!

In the end, BLUE won! Now we're tied with the Sealed Envelopes. Also, sorry if all this camp speak is gibberish. It was for me my first summer. Now I'm almost fluent, though.

Love,
Bobby

P.S. Sorry Elizabeth isn't your girlfriend anymore. Are you back on JDate?

Hi, Play Dough,

How r u? (Sorry, dumb question—I know how ur doing, and it's not good.)

I know ur sooooooo mad at me (at the Apache Relay u didn't even cheer for me when I creamed tattletale Jamie in jacks), but can we talk? U should know my side of the story.

I thought of someplace adventurous to meet, because that's ur strength as Lieutenant. Also it's a place ur trapped to listen to me explain myself . . .

Trambopoline @ 10 p.m. Be there. Or I'll be bouncing alone like a loser ☹.

XO,
Jenny

Jumping to Conclusions

Jenny sat cross-legged on the trambopoline—the trampoline in the lake—looking up at the stars. One shot by in the corner of her eye, and she wondered if it was a sign that whatever was left of her hopes and dreams was about to explode and die.

She heard a *tap, tap, tap* and bounced to her knees, hoping to see Play Dough kayaking to meet her, but it was just TJ and the Captain coming through the dock's speakers.

> **Captain:** Blue and White teams, the third day of Color War is complete! Your officers are busy preparing for SING, so TJ and I will get straight to the scores.
>
> **TJ:** I'm about to reeeee-lay some important deets. As you know, Blue earned the fourth Sealed Envelope today for the Apache Reeeee-lay!
>
> **Captain:** Very nice.
>
> **TJ:** It's all about the wordplay.
>
> **Captain:** At the moment, White and Blue have two envelopes each.
>
> **TJ:** And the sports 'n' spirit points are super-close, too, with a score of 478 and 492—Blue in the leaaaaaaad!

The Hills erupted with Blue team cheers. Jenny leapt to her feet and did a series of celebratory midair splits. Ever since her Hatchet Plan had gone awry, she'd been worried her team would suffer big-time. But no siree! They hadn't suffered at all! *B-B-L, B-L-U-E, Blue team is consequence-free!*

Captain: Those numbers are wrong.

TJ: I guess there's a reason I run a *camp* and not a *school*. Apologies, my math is as rusty as a—

Captain [*whispering*]**:** No, it's the Hatchet incident. With . . .

TJ [*whispering*]**:** Ohhh! Jenny Nolan. Right. Eesh. How do I break—?

Captain: The Hatchet Hunt is on a two-day freeze for the Blue team only. No more clues until then. We've recalculated the scores, taking both teams' penalties into account. *458* and *442*—White is in the lead.

TJ: Totally tubular.

Jenny plopped down on her butt, totally depressed. She could just imagine the chaos in Faith Hill Cabin. Jamie, Missi, and Slimey were probably popping the sparkling cider that Jamie's mom had brought on Visiting Day. Melman was probably slamming her soccer ball against her creepy Pelé poster. Sophie was probably casting some robot-vampire spell to turn Jenny into a frog.

Jenny counted her lucky stars she wasn't there. Somehow,

her excuse to Scottie—"I have to report to the HC to write apology letters, byeeeee!"—had worked. It wasn't a total lie. She did have to report to the HC to write apology letters. Just not tonight. *Tomorrow* night. Jenny figured that when tomorrow night rolled around, she would then explain to Scottie that her apology letters hadn't been apologetic enough, and she was being forced to endure Punishment Night #2.

Jenny's pink sports watch randomly beeped: 10:18. She looked toward the lonely dock and sighed. Play Dough wasn't coming. She'd slipped him a message at dinner, but it was on a paper plate, so maybe he'd just scooped egg salad on top of it and hadn't noticed. Or he was currently so deep in SING planning with his fellow officers, he couldn't sneak off. Or, more likely, he just didn't care what she had to say. She'd done enough damage to this war.

Jenny laid back down and closed her eyes. She listened to the lapping water, the trills of crickets, and the kayak bobbing against the side of the trambopoline. It was horrifically peaceful. Jenny missed cheering. She missed having her friends by her side. She missed dishing free advice. Now she didn't have a voice worth hearing. No friends to cuddle-spoon with. No fans wanting to listen to her at all. She was ready to send her mom the text she'd composed: *Pick me up from camp now pls. I have no future. Transfer all the money I have in my Homecoming Fund and Pageant Fund and Relationship Therapy Fund into a charity for friendless losers who try too hard to be something they're not.*

"Uhhh, Jenny?"

Jenny involuntarily shrieked. Then she bit her fingers to stop herself from involuntarily shrieking more. "Play Dough?" She scrambled onto her hands and knees and peered over the side of the trambopoline closest to the dock.

"I'm on the other side," Play Dough croaked. She crawled to the other side, where he stood trembling on a surf bike.

Jenny smiled. "You came!"

"Can you tie it up?" Play Dough asked. "This is hard on my glutes."

"Sure." Jenny tied the surf bike to the kayak. "All set."

Play Dough leapt toward the trambopoline. He belly flopped halfway on, kicked his legs hard for momentum, and clawed at the jumping pad in front of him. Jenny used all of her strength to pull him to safety. She grunted between yanks: "You know. There's. A. Ladder. Right?"

"I forgot." His whole body now on board, Play Dough flipped onto his back, wheezing. "Oh boy. Oh boy. Oh boy."

Jenny just stared at him, her hands on her hips. She wanted him to stop hyperventilating and to give her an *I forgive you* bear hug. But, understandably, a hug wasn't in the cards. At least not until Jenny explained herself.

"Why'd you do it?" Play Dough sat up, as cross-legged as his chubby legs would cross. "Why'd you try to get me in trouble? Why'd you try to make me look like an idiot? Are you trying to make the Blue team lose?!"

"I didn't mean to," Jenny said. She took a quick breath, about to launch into the apologetic/inspirational/motivational speech she'd prepared.

"Why'd. You. Do. It?" Play Dough cut in, slamming his fists on the jumping pad like an ill-tempered toddler.

Jenny wobbled. She looked at Play Dough's face, which was wrinkled in stress, and she knew she'd have to save her elaborate speech for another time. "The truth is, I had no idea where the Hatchet was. I'm clueless when it comes to clues. But I knew that if I got the White team disqualified, then we'd have more time to find the Hatchet."

"Uhhh."

"I assumed Jamie and Missi would snoop in my diary, so I wrote down that the Hatchet was hidden in the Captain's golf cart. Then I stole the groundskeeper's Hatchet, decorated it, and hid it under the golf cart seat cushion. Missi and Jamie were supposed to find it and present it to the Captain, who'd be like 'Um, you trespassed. Also this is a fake. Also, you're disqualified.'"

Play Dough shook his head, confused. "So where did I fit into this brilliant plan of yours? What was the point of us even being there?"

"Well, Jamie and Missi would've totally ratted me out. I needed you to think that I had nothing to do with the Fake Hatchet, so if they tried to blame me, you'd defend me to the Captain."

"So, basically, you lied to my face."

Yup, Jenny thought guiltily. She hadn't really thought about how mean her plan was to Play Dough when she was planning it. Not to mention, it was totally flawed. "It was dumb, Play Dough. I guess I just wanted to see it all play out, but we should have stayed clear of Hill Hall. That would have made a better alibi."

"So, what you're saying is that you used me but you wish you'd used me differently, so you wouldn't be in trouble?" Play Dough asked.

"Kind of." Jenny picked at the jumping pad, thinking of Willamena and how effortless it was for her to stay on top. But for Jenny, it seemed like the more she tried to be the Best, the worse she became.

"You know that doesn't make it any better, right?"

Jenny felt herself wanting to open up. Play Dough had that effect on her. "Honestly, I think I convinced myself I was using you for our benefit. I would give us more time to find the Hatchet. But now I see it both ways." She laughed apologetically, hoping Play Dough would join her, and all their tenseness would evaporate into the starry night.

But Play Dough didn't laugh. He got up and jump-stomped around the edge of the jumping pad. "I thought you'd changed."

Jenny stumbled, embarrassed. "I'm sorry—I shouldn't have gotten you involved."

"NO DUH!" he screamed.

Jenny's open heart clamped shut. "But in my defense, you weren't supposed to charge the golf cart and steal the Hatchet from Missi and Jamie. I literally told you to stop."

"I thought they were being mean to you! I was trying to stand up for you!"

"That's exactly why I thought my plan would work."

"There was no plan."

"Um, yes, we talked about it."

"No, YOU talked about it." Play Dough stopped stomping and straight-up jumped. "You tricked me into thinking you were looking out for your best friends." He jumped more angrily. "You tricked me into thinking you knew where the Hatchet was." He jumped even more angrily. "I ditched my friends for you!"

Jenny kept both hands flexed to her sides for balance, but it wasn't working so well. She wobbled in every direction. "I'm seriously sorry! The scheme was mean!"

"You're right. Dover and Smelly were right. All you do is think of yourself." Play Dough jumped again. Jenny toppled forward. "Now we'll never find the Hatchet." He jumped higher. Jenny bounced and crashed to the pad. "I'll never be a good Lieutenant!" He jumped super-high. "I'LL FAIL EVERYONE!"

Jenny went flying. Everything felt like it was in slow motion. The wind whipped. Her stomach flipped. The stars blurred together into bedazzled streaks. She hoped Play Dough would catch her, but as she contorted in the air, she saw him staring helplessly. His mouth was hanging so open, a whole loaf of lake bread could've fit inside. *Please don't let me land in the scary, black water*, Jenny prayed to the Color War Gods. *Please, no!*

And then they answered her prayers. Jenny bounced off the edge of the trambopoline, bounced *again* onto another part of the edge, and right before her toes hit the lake, Play Dough grabbed her by the waist. Jenny gripped the protective cushioning over the springs, totally traumatized. As Play Dough tugged her to the middle of the jumping pad, Jenny accidentally un-Velcroed the cushioning.

"Are you OK?!" Play Dough asked, his voice cracking with guilt.

And that's when Jenny saw it, tucked inside the exposed springs. *No way. NO. WAY.* She tried to string a sentence together, but her tongue was bloated with shock.

"Uhhh, Jenny?"

She crawled toward it and pointed. "L-l-look." She was afraid her near-lake experience was making her see stuff that wasn't there. "Do you see what I see?"

Play Dough butt-shuffled over to the springs. His whole body tensed up like how it did when bees buzzed around him. "Nah, it can't be. Can it?"

Trembling, Jenny reached toward a blue-and-white-striped rag stuffed between two of the springs. She wriggled it free. Underneath was the Hatchet.

She retreated in disbelief. Play Dough guffawed. Jenny guffawed louder. Play Dough bounced to standing. Jenny bounced to standing. They looked at each other and then back at the prized Hatchet wedged safely in the springs and screamed. "AHHHHHHHHHHHHHH!"

"We found it, uh! We found it, uh!" Play Dough chanted, taking the rag from Jenny and whipping it in the air.

"WE FOUND IT, UH, WE FOUND IT!" they chanted together.

They tried to make up something to sing in unison, but it turned into a hilarious, messy overlap of words: *"THE HATCHET . . . IS . . . RATCHET . . . BUT WE CATCHED IT, UH UH UH!"*

"We have to be quieter!" Jenny squealed, overwhelmed with giggles.

"Dude-a-cris!" Play Dough said. "I can't!"

"We're not even allowed to find the Hatchet for two more days!"

"So let's put the rag back over it and get it later," Play Dough suggested. "Deal?"

"Deal!" Jenny cried. Literally, she was so overwhelmed with joy, the tears were zigzagging down her face.

Play Dough began to twirl Jenny. She should have been able to move gracefully—she had seventeen dance trophies at home—but she was stumbling as if she'd just done a dozen dizzy Izzys. Finally, when they were too light-headed and exhausted to bounce around anymore, they collapsed onto the jumping pad and breathed heavy, happy breaths. "I didn't mean to hurt you," Jenny said, really hoping that this time the apology would stick.

"I believe you—what you said," he told her. "And I believe in you, too."

Something came over Jenny. Her stomach was vibrating with newly birthed butterflies. Her cheeks were buzzing. Her toes were curling. The stars above were strobing. The crickets were scoring a Taylor Swift symphony. And then, before she could judge herself, her lips locked onto Play Dough's lips.

ROPE BURN RULES
1.
The ropes get dipped in the lake before the burn.
2.
Each team gets three matches and a starter pile of logs, twigs, and leaves, oh my!
3.
All collected wood must no longer be growing, but must still be in its natural state. No burning wood chairs!
4.
Only fire—no wood—can touch the rope. We can't send you home with a hook for a hand.
5.
The team whose fire breaks their rope first wins.

Rope Burn

"ROPE BURN TIIIIIIIIIME!" TJ bellowed into a megaphone.

At the eighth hole of the Rolling Hills golf course, Play Dough stood with the Blue officers in front of their Rope Burn station: a thick rope strung between two ten-foot-tall metal poles. Below the rope was where the fire would be built.

Play Dough was getting goose bumps just being so close to where the Rope Burn tradition launched over fifty years ago. Gramps Garfink was Color War General that first summer and loved to tell the story of how he'd started his team's fire by farting into a lighter. Great-Uncle Garfink loved to tell his story about how the fire burned off his hair and he'd been bald ever since. Aunt Denise's Rope Burn experience was absolutely epic-sauce. It had downpoured for three days straight, so all of the logs were soaked and not catching fire. She'd raced to the HC for a nine-volt battery and a paper clip and then forged a tinder nest from all the dried-up plants in the abandoned Nature Shack. Four hours, twenty-one minutes, and eight seconds later, their rope broke . . . and they won. And to cap it all off, in 1985, as General, Pops had set the record for the fastest burn: thirty-one minutes flat!

So even though Play Dough was no Eagle Scout like Dover and no athlete like Smelly, he was a natural when it came to nurturing a spark. He had told General Power his history, hoping the General would promote him from Log Fetcher to Fire Builder, but he'd just patted Play Dough on the back like Play Dough was out of his scorched mind. Then he'd disregarded the Officer's Only rule and invited Dover to advise with the Highgate Lieutenants. Meanwhile on White, Steinberg had slipped Totle some magical equation that Wiener kept bragging was the "Pythagorean Theorem of Rope Burning." No Blue officer would admit to feeling rattled, but they'd all seen Steinberg explode stuff enough times to know he wasn't just running his mouth.

But none of this bothered Play Dough as much as he thought it would. He was still going to be a part of Rope Burn just like his Pop and Aunt Denise and Great-Uncle Garfink and Gramps. He'd still be able to prove his worth tomorrow when he and Jenny revealed the Hatchet. Oh, and the biggest reason he was feeling unbothered was that he was In Love. Big time Love. The kind of Love that fills you up more than a crème brûlée. A Love so all-consuming, it was hard for Play Dough to focus on anything other than the taste of Jenny's cherry ChapSticked lips. So, sure, Rope Burn was insanely thrilling, but what bigger fire was there than the one burning in his heart?

Play Dough cracked a few twigs from the starter woodpile at his feet and replayed the kiss in his head for the thousandth time. They'd found the Hatchet and jumped for joy. Play Dough had collapsed, and Jenny had collapsed next to him, her smooth hairless arm touching his smooth hairless arm. Then, before his heart had a chance to settle down, Jenny's face had crept over his face. He'd opened his mouth to ask her about it, but then his lips had gotten the answer. For six. Whole. Seconds. His response? His whole body had melted like a sizzling hunk of butter on a frying pan. Being only thirteen, Play Dough knew he'd only had a couple of monumental moments—his bar mitzvah and the first time he'd tasted cake—but this was by far the MOST monumental. It was something he'd tell their grandkids about.

TJ stepped in front of the eighth-hole flag, which was staked between the two Rope Burn stations. "Welcome, Blue and White. There's no more perfect way to polish off Day Four of Color War than with the annual Rope Burn competition! I challenge you to find the rhyme scheme in that sentence. Please take a seat." Some of the girls had the forward thinking to bring towels and lawn chairs, but mostly everyone just plopped on their butts on the freshly sprinklered grass. "Now RISE TO YOUR FEET and give it up for your Color War officers. They're about to birth a KILLER FIIIIIIRE!"

Both teams leapt to their feet and began screaming for their Generals and Lieutenants. Play Dough listened for his name—surely Jenny, wherever she was, was cheering for him. But he only heard chants for Dover and Melman. The orange sky was darkening, so he squinted at the rows of Blue to spot her.

After last night's fit of passion, Play Dough had snuck off to the Arts & Crafts shack and ironed HATCHET HERO onto a Blue T-shirt that he'd snatched from the Shirt Donation Box in the tie-dye nook. The letters had turned out a little crooked, and there were no more iron-on *C*s or *H*s, so he'd Sharpied those letters in. But still, he hoped she liked it when he presented it to her tomorrow.

Play Dough had wanted to make the shirt for her, but it had also been an excuse to avoid Hamburger Hill Cabin until his friends were asleep. Dover was still ranting about how "bros who chose Hatchets didn't know how to hack it." Smelly kept doing that thing where he smiled tolerantly at Play Dough, which to everyone who knew him meant he had something totally intolerant brewing in his neurotic head. Plus, surely Totle, Steinberg, and Wiener were celebrating White's lead with shaving cream beards. And the main reason he couldn't have just gone straight back to the bunk: He would have blurted out that he'd just gotten to first with Jenny Nolan.

Now, this was something he proudly wanted to blurt. Heck, he wanted to holler a play-by-play from the rooftop of Hamburger Hill Cabin! But Totle would have whipped out his journal to write it all down. Wiener would have salivated over the deets, and then turned the whole thing into a Q&A about macking Missi. Smelly would have said something about how girls don't like it when you brag about getting with them. Dover would have pointed out that Play Dough was an even bigger hack than he'd thought. And Steinberg would have probably gone quiet with PTSD from all the times he'd shoved peanut butter in his mouth to avoid Sophie's tongue. And the final reason Play Dough had kept his cherry Chapsticked lips sealed: He didn't want to ruin it with Jenny. If the guys knew that he'd snuck off with her to the trambopoline after the officers' meeting, that would have meant more points off for Blue, his demotion from Lieutenant, and no Hatchet co-find.

TJ shouted into the megaphone: "All right, all right, you spirited beasts, listen up. The Rope Burn will begin in three minutes. Generals, finalize strategies with your Fire Builders. Everyone else, dance it out!" He clapped twice, and Billy Joel's "We Didn't Start the Fire" blasted from giant speakers on either side of the Rope Burn stations.

For the third time, Play Dough scanned the crowd for Jenny. He spotted Sophie, her fingers like peace signs, violently jabbing the air. Two rows back was Smelly, waving his arms over his head. On the White team's side, Missi and Wiener were holding hands, doing the snake wave. Steinberg had one hand over an ear and the other pretending to spin tunes. Slimey was doing the running man. Where was Jenny?

Prickly spikes tickled Play Dough's shoulder. He stumbled backward and saw what he'd brushed against: Jamie's hair-sprayed head. He guessed it made sense that Jamie was beside him. As their team's Log Fetchers, once TJ blew his whistle, they'd both be sorting through the starter pile to hand flammables off to their runners, Melman and Totle. But still, he wished she weren't standing so close. The last time he'd seen her, they were wrestling in the Captain's golf cart over a weapon that could have hacked their faces off. Luckily, Play Dough was feeling extra confident today, so he brushed that aside. "Do you know where Jenny is?" he asked.

Jamie spun around, frightened. He guessed she hadn't realized her white spiky hair had been all up on his shoulder. Probably because she didn't have any peripheral vision—she was wrapped in white Ace bandages head to stomach. As far as Play Dough knew, Jamie hadn't become a burn victim in the last thirty-six hours, so it was probably for protection from tonight's fire. "She's in the HC, getting punished," she answered.

Play Dough's heart ached a little. "Oh."

"Sorry she used you, too."

Play Dough grinned. He realized grinning was a strange reaction. He understood what Jamie meant and agreed. It was just that Jamie looked like a gerbil mummy, and that tickled him.

"What's so funny?" Jamie asked. "Why are you smiling like that?"

Play Dough took a breath and refocused. His mind had slipped back to Jenny's lips. "Maybe she did use us, but I don't get why you'd snoop in her diary after you two made up." It was something that had been bothering him anyway. If Jamie and Missi had just minded their own business, the whole Hatchet fiasco would have been fiasco-free.

"'Made up'?" Jamie echoed. "We never made up."

Play Dough scrunched his nose in confusion. "Jenny said you guys made up."

"No," Jamie said. "And I snooped in her diary because she ranked our whole cabin. Like how good and bad we are at stuff for Color War. She gave me the saddest score ever and herself a completely perfect one. She's a mean, deluded person, Play Dough."

Play Dough's pining heart felt like it was being upstaged by gas pains. He didn't quite know what to do with all of that information. Sure, Jenny's plan had sucked, but she'd for real apologized to him. Maybe once Jamie got her apology, she'd feel better, too. Plus, even if Jenny sometimes *acted* mean and deluded, that wasn't who she was deep inside. He could see that. "Well, maybe cut her some slack. She's going through a really tough time with Christopher."

"Omigod, she used that excuse on you, too?" Jamie asked. "She just wants attention."

"I saw the letter before she ripped it up."

"What letter?"

"From Christopher."

"OK, but what letter from Christopher?"

"The one where he broke up with her."

"They broke up?"

"She didn't tell you?"

"She told YOU?" Jamie's face wrinkled up like she was going to sneeze. Play Dough didn't know if she was sad or angry or having an allergy attack. Maybe all three. She started striding away.

"Where are you going?" Play Dough asked. "Don't you have to Log Fetch in a minute?"

Jamie swiveled on her heels to face him. "Are you brainwashed?!" she hissed. "She knows you've liked her for forever. And she's using that to get you to do whatever she wants. Don't be a puppet, Play Dough."

"I'm not a puppet," he croaked.

"I was her puppet for so many years, and I wish someone had cut the strings. She wants you on her side because she has no one else. She wants you on her side because you're the closest to Lieutenant that she'll ever be. She wants you on her side so that you'll defend her to me, just like you're doing now."

Play Dough retreated into another replay of last night's magic. But it wasn't a romance he was seeing. It was a psychological thriller. He rewound to the moment before they'd found the Hatchet. Play Dough had been yelling, super-angry. Jumping with the opposite of joy. Because she *had* used him. She'd betrayed him. And maybe her apology and her sorry act was just another one of her sucky plans. She'd kissed him, but did that mean she'd changed into a better person? Did that mean she was truly sorry? Had she put the moves on him just so that he'd forget all about why he'd been mad at her in the first place?

Jamie peeled some of the bandage from her forehead. "Also, if Jenny told you about Christopher before she told me, she must be having a psychotic breakdown."

Play Dough could feel his face getting warm with embarrassment, his heart plummeting through the folds of his belly. Johnny Cash's "Ring of Fire" was playing now: *"I fell into a burnin' ring of fire / I went down, down, down."* The perfect score to his misery.

Suddenly, Melman was beside him. "You ready?" she asked, smiling ear to ear. Play Dough was numb in the throat, so he nodded weakly. Totle arrived, too, and fist-bumped Jamie. She halfheartedly fist-bumped him back.

TJ cut the music, and everyone went silent. "Attention, Blue and White. The Generals have informed me that they're all set. Which is good. Because the three minutes are up." He pointed his megaphone at Play Dough and Jamie. "Log Fetchers: On your mark, get set—" He blew his whistle.

The whole camp burst into cheers. The Roots' "The Fire" began blasting. Play Dough anticipated an adrenaline rush, but indifference clotted his heart. He went through the motions of handing Melman logs and then twigs and then leaves. He tried to let the chanting and music fuel him, but it all hummed into white noise.

When the starter pile ran low, Play Dough jogged two holes north to the woodsy edge of the golf course to snag more branches. His brain was telling him to collect wood *faster, faster, faster*, but his fingers were fumbling and his legs felt like tree trunks. Finally, he slapped himself and his brain won out. He grabbed as much material as he could hold in the fold of his shirt and in the garbage bag he'd slung over his shoulder. He hustled back to the Rope Burn site, where White had a licking ball of fire halfway to their rope and Blue had diddly.

White was roaring: *"BUILD THAT FIRE, HIGHER, HIGHER!"* Totle was wet with sweat and smiling all deranged. Jamie was probably wet with sweat underneath her mummy getup. The White team officers were surrounding the fire, watching it grow. On the sidelines, Wiener had a Bunker Hiller on his shoulders and Steinberg was shouting fractions.

Play Dough shifted his gaze to Blue's station. Dover was ranting about stick rubbing because the wind had smothered all three of their matches. The Lieutenants were scrambling to copy White's triple-hashtag log formation. General Power had somehow burned his hand and was hopping around, cursing himself.

It hit him: Play Dough had to step in. He ran to the entrance of the golf course and snatched two fistfuls of hay from a decorative haystack. Then he rushed into the Golf Shack, where he snagged a nine-volt battery and a paper clip from a desk drawer. He sprinted back with all of his supplies.

"Knot this together with some dry leaves," he told Melman, giving her the hay. He handed Dover the nine-volt battery and the clip. "When Melman's done, rub this paper clip on both battery terminals at the same time." He faced General McCarville. "General, get your Lieutenants to huddle together—we need to contain the wind." He'd have given General Power something to do, but he was off to the side, getting his hand anointed by Nurse Nanette.

In their General's absence, no Blue officer thought twice about following Play Dough's orders. Melman knotted, Dover waited to rub, and the rest huddled around Play Dough as he reconfigured the double hashtag into a tepee of sticks inside a bigger tepee of logs inside an even bigger tepee of branches. Melman placed the tinder nest inside the smallest tepee. Dover rubbed the clip to the battery. It sparked. A baby fire was born. Then Play Dough threw himself wherever the wind was blowing. Once the fire was toddler-size, he cried: "De-huddle!"

The Lieutenants de-huddled and their fire was revealed for all to see. Blue began screaming: *"B-U-R-N, BUUUUURN THE ROPE!"* A new song played, the lyrics: *"Burn, baby, burn, disco inferno,"* and all of Blue was singing along. White kept darting looks over to their opponent's station. Their cheering simmered as Blue's fire outflamed theirs.

Over the next half hour, Play Dough and his fellow officers fed and fanned their fire. They dodged embers and pulled their shirts up over their noses to avoid the smoke. Play Dough got so sweaty he might as well have emerged from the lake. White's fire had since gained height—their officers had fed and fanned it just like Blue. From the sidelines, the teams looked neck and neck. But Play Dough noted a major difference between the two apex flames: Blue's was focused on the middle of the rope; White's was frolicking two inches in front. He knew which was better even if no one else did.

Suddenly, Blue's screams escalated and the hills shook. Pat Benatar's "Fire and Ice" shot through the dark. Blue team's rope had caught on fire. *"THE ROPE, THE ROPE, THE ROPE IS ON FIRE!"* they chanted on repeat.

Play Dough stood still for the first time in nearly an hour, watching Blue's rope sizzle black and thin to floss. There was nothing more he could do, so he took Melman's hand and General McCarville's hand and awaited the fate of the fire.

Twelve seconds later, Blue's rope broke.

Summer of Love

Jenny sat in a beanbag chair in the HC, chewing on her pink pen cap. Across from her sat the Captain at her desk, plugging away on her laptop. They'd been sitting in boring office land for over an hour now, and Jenny was about to tear her silky strands out. She was three hills away from the Rope Burn and suffering from the worst case of FOMO imaginable.

Jenny had always pictured herself a Rope Burn star, costumed like Katniss Everdeen in *Catching Fire*. So it was kind of sad that not only was she barred from the event of the summer, but she was locked away with the Captain. The whole punishment was seriously torching her vibe. She didn't want to write sorry letters to Jamie and Missi. She wanted to grow the fire between her and Lieutenant "Peeta" Play Dough, who, like the real Peeta, was really into bread.

"How are your apologies coming, Jenny?"

"Really good," Jenny lied.

"Your stationery is blank," the Captain pointed out.

Jenny looked down at her stationery bordered with hearts and lipstick kisses. "Ugh." It was hard to write an apology to her ex-BFF on smoochy paper when whatever love was once between them was now burnt to a crisp. "Do you have any stationery with skulls on them?"

"No."

"How about spiders?"

"Why would I have that?"

"UGGGGGGGH."

The Captain passed Jenny a "To-Do List" notepad. It was mustard brown with ugly bubble bullet points.

"Perfect, thanks!" Jenny put her pen to the paper, but nothing but doodles came out. Her first two apology letters had been so easy. She'd filled the one to Eddie with compliments on his Hatchet and advice on how to redecorate the Tool Shed. (More shades of pink, less opossum poop.) The one to Missi had been a little more challenging. Jenny had been able to write nice things about Missi's sense of curiosity and how her hair was just so full of life, but she'd crossed all of her toes in the process. After all, Missi was nothing but a Best Friend Stealer.

By now, her energy was sucked dry and she didn't have it in her heart to say nice things to Jamie. Jenny decided that she should just be honest. She stopped doodling and got to work:

~~To-Do List:~~ (Apology Letter to Jamie)

Dear Jamie,

- Sorry u hate me.

Jenny

"Ta-da!" Jenny handed the letter over to the Captain for approval.

The Captain scanned it, lifted her glasses to the top of her head, and rubbed her eyes. "I was hoping you'd write something encouraging. Jamie is your best friend, right?"

Jenny tilted her head in consideration, halfway between a yes and a no. Jamie *had* been her best friend. But that was before she stopped supporting Jenny, and quit caring about Jenny's relationship with Christopher, and made mash-up names with Missi. Jenny spit out the pen cap that she'd been chewing. It was the consistency of taffy. "Can I ask you a question?"

"Go ahead," the Captain said.

"Were you forced to pick Jamie for Lieutenant or was it a mistake? Like, did her mom bribe you or something? Francine Nederbauer has serious helicopter parenting issues."

The Captain gently closed her laptop and folded her arms on her desk. "TJ and I did not accept a bribe. We did not make a mistake. We chose Jamie on purpose."

Jenny wrinkled her nose in disbelief. "Why?"

"Jamie never gets a chance to shine. I wanted to give her that chance," the Captain explained. "She's shining now, Jenny. You see that, don't you?"

Jenny shrugged. She guessed Jamie had come into her own these last few days. But she'd also become a power-hungry monster.

The Captain got up and stretched. Then she walked to her super-serious filing cabinet. Jenny assumed she was going to pull out some infographic charting Jamie's shine factor, but instead she removed a bag of trail mix. She offered Jenny some—Jenny picked out two raisins and a carob chip. The Captain continued: "I think Jamie's stepping into her leadership role, just like you've done every summer with Miss Rolling Hills and Campstock and the intercamp dance competitions. I see a lot of you in her now."

Jenny bulged her eyes. She knew the Captain meant that as a compliment, but she couldn't also help but think that meant Jenny was a power-hungry monster, too, and that she'd bred Jamie's meanness. Maybe Jamie was her Frankenstein baby, just like she'd become Willamena's. It hurt her heart to think about it, so she took a two-second nap and refocused. "Can I move on to the next letter?"

The Captain sighed. "For now." Then she threw back a handful of trail mix and returned to her laptop.

Jenny had been dreading writing this final letter. She didn't need to apologize to Play Dough—their differences had been settled when they'd smooched. So what was she supposed to write? That her heart felt as gooey as a campfired marshmallow? That he'd triggered a million hyperactive butterflies in her belly? That kissing him felt more special than it had ever felt with Christopher?

Absolutely not. Jenny was Jenny. Play Dough was Play Dough. What would her followers think? Willamena and Riley and the rest of her school and dance friends? Her camp friends? Surely they would think that her rebound was a charity case. That she was having her celebrity meltdown five years too soon. Jenny had considered keeping their make-out a secret, but with her high profile and Play Dough's conspicuous body, it would only be a matter of time before it leaked. Everyone in her life would stop believing she'd ever had what it takes to be Lieutenant and Head Cheerleader and Homecoming Queen and Miss Everything. That is, if they hadn't stopped believing in her already.

"Jenny, are you OK?"

Jenny shook out of her daymare and looked down at her lap: the note was covered in doodled hearts and *Mrs. Jenny Garfink* signatures. She threw her hand over it, embarrassed. "Do I have to write this one?" she asked. "Can't I just go to Rope Burn and apologize to Play Dough in person?"

"You're with me until Taps."

"Ugh. Why couldn't I have gotten punished yesterday?!"

"Sorry about that," the Captain said. "It was our twentieth anniversary. TJ and I wanted to celebrate."

Jenny perked up. Maybe she and the Captain could gossip about married life until Taps (aka the bedtime bugle). Then Jenny wouldn't have to process her unruly emotions after all. "OK, tell me everything!" she squealed.

The Captain laughed. "What would you like to know?"

"Was it love at first sight?"

The Captain snorted and then covered her smiling mouth.

"What's so funny?"

"Well, TJ and I weren't the most likely couple. He was a goofy soccer specialist who lived in the moment, and I was a head lifeguard with dreams of the navy. TJ had never had a girlfriend, and I'd had my fair share of relationships. TJ was nineteen, and I was twenty-two. I was ready to buckle down with someone mature. TJ was the opposite of mature!"

Jenny grinned. She could totally picture a silly nineteen-year-old TJ and a super-mature twenty-two-year-old pre-navy Captain interacting like complete aliens, stumbling over their words and sharing their first super-awk kiss! Aw! "So what happened? How'd he win you over?"

"He didn't."

Jenny cocked her chin.

"*I* won *him* over."

"You did?!" Jenny cried. "Why?"

The Captain sighed happily. "The heart wants what the heart wants."

Jenny's mind leapt to Play Dough. Something clicked hard. "Like, love just finds you in the most unexpected places, right?"

"Exactly," the Captain said.

Jenny beamed, but she didn't want to be so obvious about her feelings. "I want to be a relationship therapist when I get older, so this is really good to know." And then it hit her that, sure, the heart is free to love whomever, but what about what the rest of the world thinks? "Wait, so did you, like, lose your whole fan base?" Jenny asked.

"Sorry?"

"Like your friends, and family, and everyone on social media, if the Internet was a thing back then?"

The Captain smirked. "Everyone who loved me was thrilled—said I could use a goofball in my life. And everyone in TJ's life was thrilled, too—he needed someone practical with lifelong goals. We were good for each other, and twenty summers later, we still are. In fact, Psychedelic Sixties and Awesome Eighties were the Color War themes the summer we were Generals together. We revived the themes this summer as a sort of anniversary gift to each other."

"It's the summer of love," Jenny swooned.

"I guess it is."

Totally randomly, Jenny's sight went blurry. She dabbed her eye, and a tear flew down her cheek. The Captain's love story was just so touching! Suddenly, the million butterflies in Jenny's belly fluttered awake. All she wanted to do was kiss Play Dough and taste his pepperoni breath. She didn't even eat pepperoni! What was happening to her body?! Maybe Jenny was done with the Prince Hanses out there, because she had found her Kristoff. Maybe the stars were aligning. Maybe it didn't matter what was in her followers' hearts, just hers. Her true friends had to understand. And if they didn't, maybe they weren't her true friends after all. "Sorry, I have to— I think I can write my letter now."

Jenny tossed the Captain's "To-Do List" notepad at her feet and pulled her hearts and lipstick kisses stationery to her lap. She gave her romantic life one final thought: In a heated moment, when love overpowered anger, Play Dough had held Jenny in his pudgy arms, made her giggle, and wiped their slate clean with the sweetest kiss. What more could she possibly want?

Jenny put her pen to paper, and this time, the letter wrote itself.

Gaining Momentum

TJ: Wow. What a burn this summer! With us tonight are our Generals, minutes after the Rope Burn of the century!

Captain: Who won?

General McCarville: *B-B-L, B-L-U-E, Psychedelic Sixties to victory!*

TJ: Well, let's hear those rhymes! White, you're uuuuuup!

General Ferrara: Tonight's burn was a total thrill / Steinberg's formula was utterly brill.

General Silver: Our rope came to break just seconds behind / A more resilient team you'll never find!

TJ: Niiiice. And representing Blue will just be General McCarville. General Power is in the infirmary getting his hand glued back on.

Captain: TJ, the children!

TJ: Hi, children!

General McCarville: Blazing dreams, our fiery Blues / Kick off those love beads and soak in the news / Our MVP tonight did not give a stink! / Let's give it up for Play Dough Garfink!!!

TJ: Garfink in the Hamburger Hoouuuuuuse! The current scores are: 503 points, two Sealed Envelopes—White. 589 points, three Sealed Envelopes—Blue. Sweet dreams!

"PLAY DOUGH'S ARMY!" Dover and Smelly chanted. *"PLAY DOUGH'S ARMY!"*

Play Dough was up on his teammates' shoulders, about to make the grandest of grand entrances into Hamburger Hill Cabin. He was six feet from the ground but felt on top of the world.

"My back. Ow." Dover cringed. "My back."

"I think," Smelly started. "I think my shoulder is coming out of its socket."

Play Dough pressed his palms to the top of their heads for better balance and also encouragement. "Guys, two porch steps and we're at the door."

The guys pushed forward, and Play Dough fumbled with the doorknob. Finally, they made their grand entrance, chanting: *"PLAY DOUGH'S ARMY!"* They were met by Steinberg on Totle's and Wiener's shoulders, chanting: *"STEINBERG EQUALS MC SQUARED!"* The Blue and White Hamburgers were like mirror images of each other, and the pure coincidence of it made them stop in their tracks and break into laughter.

"Don't move!" Yoshi called, scrambling to get his heavy-duty camera.

Steinberg froze his whole body mid-laugh as a joke. Play Dough dug up some earwax and touched it to Steinberg's nose.

"Dude-a-wax, no!" Steinberg cried, unfreezing and smacking his nose clean.

Yoshi fiddled with the lens and the focus and the angle and the flash. "Just hold it! This moment is too good."

Play Dough and Steinberg obeyed Yoshi for a second. But then Steinberg sneezed. To avoid getting sprayed, Play Dough lunged from Smelly's and Dover's shoulders into a pile of dirty socks. Steinberg toppled on top of him, and they fake-wrestled until Steinberg called time-out to take a puff of his inhaler. Play Dough took a puff, too, just to get the taste of stinky socks out of his mouth.

"Oh well," Yoshi said. "I guess we'll have to rely on memory."

"The memory that Hamburger Hill is dominating this war," Totle said. "Play Dough and Steinberg both got shout-outs!"

"You really turned things around, PD," Dover said. "Mad props."

"Thanks, Dov."

"General Power's got nothing on you now. He says another doubtful-poutful thing about you, and I'll be like 'No one messes with my boy, PD. He's a fire sensation is what's up!'"

"I second that," Smelly said. "How'd you even know how to start a fire like that? YouTube?"

Play Dough smiled. "Let's just say it's in my blood."

"Blood," Steinberg repeated. "Cool."

Dover threw his Eagle Scout sash over Play Dough's head. "You should join us. Work your way up to Eagle Scout like me."

Play Dough cocked his head in consideration. "Do you sell cookies like the girls?"

"No, dude. Fertilizer."

"Is it edible?"

"Not sure. It's poop, though. So probably not. But do you know what *is* edible?" Dover climbed to his top bunk and tore through his underwear cubby. He whipped out a can of Cheez Whiz. "I saved this for a special occasion!"

"CHEEZ WHIZ!" Play Dough cried. "Oh, how I've dreamed of you!" Ever since he ran out two weeks ago, he'd been craving it on the quarter hour.

The guys gathered around Dover as he sprayed cheese toward their mouths. Most of it landed on their faces and in their hair and on the beds behind them, so Yoshi stepped in. "All right, guys, let's put the can of—"

"ROPE BURN COLOGNE!" Wiener interrupted, suddenly emerging from the bathroom. Play Dough hadn't even realized he wasn't part of the Cheez Whiz mosh pit. "Guys. The sweet smell of campfire 'n' competition year-round. We make this, we'll be billionaires! Steinberg, how can we capture its essence in a bottle?"

"Rope divided by burn equals cologne," Steinberg joked.

"No, c'mon, really."

"I know!" Dover cried. "Come close."

Wiener obeyed, and Dover cheesed him in the face.

The guys melted with laughter.

There was a knock at the cabin door. The guys instantly hushed, thinking it was the Captain doing noise control. But then Jenny's face peered in through the window, her hands cupped around her eyes. Everyone seemed to sigh with relief. Except for Play Dough. He threw himself against the cabin wall, out of Jenny's sight.

"Pssst. Play Dough!" she called, not actually whispering at all. "I have to talk to you!"

He knew the mature thing to do would be to step outside and deal with Jenny head-on. To tell her that, if she wanted to gain cred like he had, she'd have to do it on her own. That he was done with her plans, once and for all. But he also knew that was dangerous. What if, instead of anger, all that L-O-V-E rushed back, like when his belly beckons for a third burrito, even though his brain is telling him he'll get butt-blasted with bowel bombs?

"You want to talk to her?" Yoshi mouthed, even though his eyebrows were saying it was a bad idea. Even Play Dough's counselor knew about his forever crush and how he'd gotten wrapped up in Jenny's manipulation with the Hatchet. How embarrassing.

Play Dough looked from Smelly to Dover to Steinberg to Totle to Wiener, searching for whatever advice they could quickly lend, but they were all looking to him to make the decision. Finally, Play Dough shook his head no.

So Yoshi let Jenny down with a "Play Dough's got to focus on writing tomorrow's rosters," and she left. Then Play Dough and Totle really did step out to the porch to write tomorrow's rosters. They didn't sit on opposite sides like normal. They sat side by side, with just enough room between them so they couldn't see the other's strategies.

As Play Dough began to brainstorm the next day's kicking order for Mass Kickball, and the running order for the Twelve-Hill Marathon, and the event breakdown for the Boating Regatta, he felt his body buzz with warmth. He may not have been on White like his family, but he had been chosen for Lieutenant, and he had it in him to lead his team to victory. Yesterday, he'd failed his team for the last time. He'd come too far to get sucked into any more drama.

"You're doing good," Totle said out of nowhere, his fist out for a pound.

Play Dough pounded him back. "You too, man."

August 15

Dear Moses 'n' Sam,

Something we can do in your apartment complex's courtyard: Rope Burn.

I came up with a formula:

$$\frac{\sqrt{\text{Triple Hashtag Log Formation}} \div \text{Two Matches} \geq \text{Magnifying Glass}^3}{\text{Wind+Fan} \times \text{90 degree angle (Stick Additions)} \approx \text{Rope Focus}} = \text{Burnt Rope}$$

It's good, but could use some fine-tuning. Sleep on it. We'll discuss when I'm home.

From,

Robert Steinberg

August 15

Dear Cassie,

Mom and Dad aren't making me write this letter, so read it please. Important Q: Is there a world in which Boy Scouts sell cookies, specifically Thin Mints or Samoas?

I'm trying to recruit.

Ben

15 August

Dear Little Ealing Fireflies,

Yo, yo, yo! I think our lateral sprints prepared me well for this crazy Color War event called Rope Burn. I had to run logs to a fire and then help the fire grow flaming high enough to burn and break a rope ten feet in the air!

We won, which was pretty kick-butt if you ask me. My co-Lieutenant, Play Dough, jumped in and saved the day. He was like "MAKE A TINDER NEST, WOMAN!" and I did!

Since we're the Fireflies and all, it might be cool to make a bonfire with all our weathered balls and goalie nets. As a sort of season launch!

Fire away, football heads.
#24,
Melman

BOATING REGATTA

Canoe/Paddleboat/Kayak Relay. One camper canoes to floating iceberg. Another paddleboats to trambopoline. Another kayaks back to the dock.

Surf Bike Relay. From dock, around trambopoline, and back.

Lake Obstacle Course. Surf bike to trambopoline, climb up, jump five times, jump off, swim to iceberg, climb up, jump off, surf bike back to dock.

Making *Her*story

"We gotta! We gotta! WE GOTTA WIN THE REGATTA!"

Jenny hiked down Forest Hill toward the lake, where the entire camp was assembled for the boating relays. With every step, the cheering got louder. She squinted through the masses and finally spotted Play Dough by the shore, dumping residual rainwater from a canoe. His biceps had a little bit of definition, she noticed. Also, his hair was enthusiastically flipped up today, kind of like a ramp. He looked really nice. Did she look nice?

She frantically pulled up her fringed jean shorts so they didn't sag in the butt and zipped her FAITH HILL FOREVER sweatshirt to her belly button. Her hair was in a too-tight side braid, so she pulled some strands out to make it look carefree. Her bangs were cooperating. Her legs were shaved. Her skin, she could feel, was glowing underneath the face-painted peace signs. Yes, she looked nice now, too.

Jenny had gone to bed last night wondering why Play Dough had refused to see her, but she'd assured herself it was because of Yoshi's stupid rules, not his. If Play Dough had had his way, he'd have come out to the porch and locked lips with

Jenny all over again. Now Jenny really couldn't wait to give him the apology letter she had in her pocket and congratulate him on his newfound popularity. Play Dough had transformed. He'd saved Rope Burn. He'd become a walking legend. Her lips had gifted him the confidence he'd needed to soar. And from this Regatta on, they'd soar together.

First things first: They needed to plot the recovery of the Hatchet. The two-day freeze was over at last, and now was the time to emerge as Color War Hatcheteers! Jenny wasn't sure yet when or how they'd reveal the Hatchet, but it was obvious what would happen once they did: Jenny would hop onto Play Dough's back. He'd hold the Hatchet in the air, and she'd plant a kiss on his cheek. This would, of course, be the featured photo of the *Hilltopper*. The headline would read: "Jenny & Play Dough: Redefining 'Cutest Camp Couple' and Inspiring Fat Boys Everywhere." Jenny "Hatcheteer" Nolan would be added to this summer's Color War plaque as an honorary Lieutenant. Her life would be back on track. And lastly, her doughy grandkids would one day feel proud generational fame.

Jenny uprooted a yellow dandelion and tucked it behind her ear. With only seven canoes between them, she locked eyes with Play Dough and waved. He looked down at his clipboard and then out to the paddleboats, pointing and counting. There were four. He didn't need to point and count. What was he doing? Jenny waved again. He counted the life jackets on the ground. There were three. Why was he counting what didn't need counting? Why hadn't he waved back? Was he nervous? Jenny thought that was just so adorable. She was nervous, too, and she couldn't wait to chat with him about how their emotions were totally in sync.

Dover's 'fro was suddenly in Jenny's line of sight, blocking her view of Play Dough's bloated, sun-kissed cheeks. "Uh, Jenny, can we talk?"

"What?"

"I have a message from Lieutenant Play Dough."

"He wants to talk to me?" she chirped. "Why didn't he say so! It's cute that he's being shy and all, but I can just go over to him, no problem." She smirked. "I know he's busy counting boats and stuff, but trust me, I'm worth it."

"Cool. So Play Dough told me to tell you that he's a free agent. Whatever you've got planned for today, you're flying solo." He spread his arms like an eagle. "Caw!"

Jenny's heartbeat grew into loud, stomping pounds. WHAT THE FLYING WHAT was Dover talking about? No way did Play Dough sanction that birdbrained message. She shoved past Dover's outstretched arm and zipped toward Play Dough, who was now dumping residual rainwater from a kayak.

Dover was stuttering to the back of her head: "Um. Jenny? Uh. Where are you—? Jenny, I don't think—!"

"Are you ready?" Jenny asked Play Dough, stepping between him and a paddleboat.

"Uh." He ducked down like he was going to tie his laces, except he wasn't wearing any—he was sporting water shoes. So he scooped around his toes. "Lodged pebble," he croaked.

Jenny chalked it up to nerves and forgave him. "Dover just said the weirdest thing to me. Like, it was funny how deranged it was."

Play Dough rose and wiped his muddy palms on his shorts.

"By the way, you look—" Jenny halted her compliment because she noticed that a part of Play Dough's tank tucked into his waistband. She went to fix it, but Play Dough stumbled back awkwardly. "What's wrong?" she asked.

"Nothing," Play Dough said. "Only Color War officers on the front lines."

"Do you mean the *shore*line?" Jenny joked with a smile.

"You'll have to take a seat on the hill like everyone else."

"But I'm not everyone else! *We're* not everyone else!"

"Huh?"

Jenny rolled her eyes. "What about"—she cupped her hands around his ear and whispered—"our Hatchet? We need to make a plan!"

Play Dough swallowed, and his Adam's apple slid up and down like a pinball. "You're welcome to get it on your own." Then he absentmindedly glanced at his clipboard and walked toward the Blue guys on the hill.

"But, wait! I have a letter for—"

The Captain blew a series of whistles from the dock and megaphoned something about the proper way to use an oar, but Jenny was too dumbstruck to listen. Instead, she threw her hood up over her head and popped a squat by Sophie, whose nose was so buried in her newest book, *1960s: What-*

a-Decade, that she was oblivious to the broken, angry heart beside her.

What the what is happening?! Jenny thought. This was not Play Dough being cutesy-nervous. This was him straight-up rejecting her. He had so much going for him now, he didn't need credit for finding the Hatchet. Nor did he desire Jenny's kisses. He was too cool and too popular and too heroic to be associated with her. Their featured photo on the *Hilltopper*? Play Dough's PR nightmare.

"Paddle, peddle, push, row. Watch out White, WE'VE GOT PLAY DOUGH!" Nearly everyone on Blue was on his or her feet, chanting.

Jenny didn't have it in her to stand, especially not to that stupid cheer, so she peeked through the Anita Hiller legs in front of her to catch the action. Apparently, the Regatta had begun. The Lauryn and Jonah Hillers were already kayaking back to the dock. The Notting Hillers and Wawel Hillers were on deck, boarding surf bikes. Play Dough was waddling back and forth on the shore, riling the crowd by wearing a life jacket as a diaper. Yes, a diaper.

You know what? Jenny thought. *I don't need to mourn the loss of this oversize baby!* She watched him do squats as the life-jacket diaper slipped to his ankles. The Blue team laughed. Some White campers couldn't contain themselves and laughed, too. Why was everyone acting so immature? This was war. Not some video gone viral. *Whatever*, Jenny thought. She didn't need to share the Hatcheteer fame. She was *Jenny Nolan*. She was the one who'd found the Hatchet in the first place. She was the one who'd planned all the plans. Katniss needed Peeta—real or not real? NOT REAL.

The whistle blew and the Captain announced a Blue win. Or maybe it was White. Jenny was so consumed with her crisis, and the teams were both cheering so wildly, she couldn't tell. Melman weaved her way to Jenny's side. "You ready to show the lake who's boss?" she asked.

Jenny had the urge to tell Melman everything. To confess that she'd found the Hatchet, and fallen in love, and had probably just gotten dumped for the second time in a week. But Melman wouldn't care about any of that except for the Hatchet part. And if she knew about the Hatchet, she'd probably "do the right thing" and rat her out about finding it after hours. Or she'd "do the wrong thing" and be complicit in Jenny's Hatchet crime. Jenny didn't want any more trouble. She just wanted a friend. But since that wasn't in the cards, she had no choice but to embrace her solo flight. "Ready, I guess."

"Great. You're doing the obstacle course. You'll surf bike to the trambopoline—"

"WHAT?"

"Just use the ladder, I have faith in you."

Jenny had thought she'd be doing the normal surf bike relay, but now Melman was telling her that she was doing the obstacle course, centimeters from the Hatchet? As she followed Melman to the dock, her mind started to spin. Could she reveal the Hatchet during the race? She knew she wasn't allowed to ditch an activity to *hunt* for the Hatchet, but like TJ had said, you're allowed to *find* it at one. And now was better than Rest

Hour, when she'd need a buddy, as per Color War rules. Because who would risk being her buddy after her last stunt? No one.

Jenny threw off her sweatshirt and shorts so she was sporting nothing but her blue tankini. She looked at Play Dough, who was on his back, detangling his ankles from the life jacket like a netted seal. She glanced at Jamie, who was helping Missi balance on a surf bike, the two of them giggling. She peeked at the spot in the trambopoline where the Hatchet was hidden, her wheels spinning faster, faster, faster.

Jenny boarded the surf bike next to a grinning Missi. "I read the letter you wrote me," Missi said.

"That's what letters are for," Jenny responded.

"Do you really think my hair is full of life?"

Jenny gave Missi a blank stare. "Uh-huh." Then she focused back on the trambopoline, her fingers gripping the bike handles so hard that her knuckles turned her opponent's color. Finally, her wheels stopped spinning. She'd settled on a plan that would earn her team a Sealed Envelope. She'd be showered with glory. She'd make camp *her*story.

The Captain roared into the megaphone: "On your surf, get set, BIKE!"

Jenny peddled as fast as she could. The water splashed up at her feet. Her heart began racing. Her bangs got damp with sweat. She soaked up Blue's singing: *"Bike, bike, bike your boat, round the trambopoline. Speedily, speedily, speedily, speedily, win it for the team!"*

Just you wait, Jenny thought, passing Missi. As her surf bike reached the trambopoline, everything seemed to happen in slow motion, just like it had the night Play Dough saved her from bouncing into the lake. Jenny launched herself onto the ladder, Missi at her heels. She climbed to the jumping pad. She jumped once, twice, three times. Missi began to jump, too. Jenny pretended to wobble backward. She fell against the protective cushioning over the springs. She reached behind her back and wriggled the rag free. Now she just had to wait for Missi to jump overboard so that she could safely grab the Hatchet and whip it in the sky!

But Missi stopped jumping. She rushed over to Jenny, grabbed Jenny's arm, and pulled her up like a good sport. At the worst time ever. "Sorry I made you fall. Let's jump off togeth—!" Missi looked at the Hatchet wedged in the springs and then back at Jenny and then back at the Hatchet. "DID WE JUST FIND THE HATCHET?!"

No, no, no, no, no! Jenny screamed to herself. She sprinted through the options in her head. (a) Grab the Hatchet and whip it high in the air *with* Missi. *No, White would earn half the credit, negating any Blue points.* (b) Pretend she hadn't understood Missi, and just jump overboard with her. *No, the next obstacle course participants would find it.* (c) Explain she'd found it first. *No one would believe her, and even if anyone did, it wouldn't help—she and Play Dough had found the Hatchet on illegal terms.*

But then Missi was going toward the Hatchet, and Jenny acted on impulse. She scrambled toward it, too. They were both holding the Hatchet now, and everyone could see. The camp was losing their minds, roaring and pointing and jumping up and down. Missi was so happy and confused she was laugh-crying. The whole thing was so unfair it was making Jenny sick. Missi had already stolen her Best Friend. Now she wanted to steal credit for finding the Hatchet, too?

Panicking, Jenny watched TJ whisper into the Captain's ear. Before either of them could announce that she and Missi were Hatchet cofinders, Jenny got so consumed with anger she couldn't think straight. The only words buzzing in her ears were Willamena's: *Anyone tries to steal my thunder, I strike them down. You've got to do what you've got to do.*

So just as the Captain moved the megaphone to her lips, Jenny yanked the Hatchet from Missi's grasp and threw it overboard.

NOOO! Jenny watched with horror and regret as the Hatchet plummeted into the lake. Then she looked at Missi, who was staring at the rippling water, the tragic aftermath, just as shocked.

There were gasps. Then silence. Then angry yelling, led by Jamie, of all people: *"Hatchet Cheater! Attention Seeker! Hatchet Cheater! Attention Seeker!"*

The lifeguards swam out to the trambopoline as quickly as they could and dove to rescue the historic Hatchet. As if it were a drowning child.

The boos came in waves so crushing, Jenny had no choice but to sit backward on the trambopoline with her hands over her ears to drown them out. She'd made *her*story, all right. And it was the worst feeling in the world.

August 16th

Dear Grandpa,

Got your present. Got your white tracksuit from the '80s. Thanks a lot! Tell Grandma that my hair might still be white when I come home. We're too busy to shower during Color War, and also, I used all three cans of hairspray on myself.

Today I almost won the obstacle course Regatta event. But I was upstaged by Jenny, who cheated again with the Hatchet.

Missi was not upstaged. She shone like a carrot in the sun.

Jamie wrote that! Big kitty cat kisses to all the cats! Pray for White—it's a close war.

Love,
Missi
+ Miss-Jam

August 16th

Dear Mom,

How are you? Color War is getting so intense! I can't believe that in just 24 hours it'll all be over ☹.

Tomorrow we are spending most of the day on SING, which is the most special part of the war. We're practicing our march and alma mater, the dancers are practicing the dance, the counselors are working on the costumes and scenery, and I'm putting the final touches on the White team's plaque. When I come home, I'll sing the songs to you and you'll probably cry—that's how beautiful and touching they are. The lyrics make you appreciate everything that's good in life ☺.

Tell Lois she's a totally ace cockatiel! (That's another 80s saying—why did people talk so weird back then? Haha!)

Love,
Stephanie

August 16

Dear Rainbow Cloud Jones,

I loved your book on Woodstock. I thought it was very compelling.

I have some questions for you:

When you said you burned your bra, was it from Target? I hope not Victoria's Secret. Their bras cost more than four gallons of stage blood.

You mentioned that you grew out your armpit hair. Cool! How many inches? Did the hair growth grow the peace movement? I'm trying to grow my eleven pit hairs out. So far, I've got a centimeter on the left and some stubborn stubble on the right.

You said you went on a lot of trips. I've gone on a lot of trips, too—to the Berkshires, Carolinas, and once, New Jersey—but never to places like the ones you described.

Your answers will make me more knowledgeable for Color Bowl, which is Color War trivia.

Also, I wish I had been born in the '60s. I think I would've fit in better then.

Your grooviest fan,
Sophie Edgersteckin

CAMP ROCKS!

Date: August 16

Dear Mom,,

How are you? I am doing a really good job as Lieutenant. Ask the Captain. But I'm not doing that good with friendships.

Camp is a mixed bag of jelly beans. Some days are very cherry when white is winning. Some days are sour cherry when I miss Jenny.

Today we won the Regatta and I called Jenny a cheater..

My favorite thing so far is the friendship I have with Missi!!!.

My cabin is kind of divided right now or maybe that's just me and Jenny.

The food is I'm eating enough, I swear.

Write back soon!

From,

Jamie

The Magic of an Alma

"Nice and loud!" General Power was on top of a chair on the basketball court, aggressively conducting his team in this summer's alma mater, set to the Beatles' 1968 hit "Hey Jude." The chair wobbled under his feet. "I CAN'T HEAR YOU, BLUE!"

Jenny rolled her eyes, sat up straight for better breath control, and obediently shout-sang:

"Hey, Blue, you've fought so well
You compel us to go out and slaughter."

The officers, except for Play Dough and a few others, who were monitoring set construction in the Social Hall, halfheartedly sang behind General Power. They looked dead-tired—puffy cheeks, twitchy eyes, fading face paint. It was clear to Jenny that they'd stayed up all night writing and fighting. And for what? The alma was TERRIBLE. Everyone knew that words like "fought" and "slaughter" were reserved for the march. The alma was supposed to make your heart go warm and fuzzy.

Having hit rock bottom yesterday, Jenny could really use some warm and fuzzy.

"LOUDER!" General Power's voice boomed into the gray sky. In the distance, a patch of dark clouds floated menacingly toward the basketball court. As if they were being beckoned to match the Blue mood.

"You bring your A-game onto the fields.
White better yield to our wicked power."

Jenny's chords went into auto-sing as her mind drifted to last summer's Color War. When she and Jamie had first sung the alma mater, they'd clutched hands after the first verse. By the chorus, their bodies had begun vibrating with emotion. By the second chorus, Missi had joined them and all vows not to cry were off. The hand-holding had gotten red-rover unbreakable, their voices had cracked, and their faces had turned into wet messes. There had been so much love in those lyrics.

"Hey, White, go on give up,
Don't try to mend what's clearly broken."

General McCarville buried her head in her hands. "Can we—?" She powered off the speaker and "Hey Jude" was silenced. Jenny perked up.

"Is there a problem?" General Power asked, stepping down.

"We need more time, Ashanti."

"More time for *what*?"

"To write." She crumbled up the lyric sheet in her hand. "The song. It's not working."

"SING is in ten hours," General Power said. "We are fighting to win."

"Singing about fighting to win will not help us win," General McCarville argued. "We need to appeal to the judges' hearts."

Jenny's head twitched back and forth between her two Generals like she was watching a US Open match point. It was awful seeing her Color War mom and dad argue. Blue was supposed to work together in harmony. The officers were supposed to take a united stand. Especially in front of the kiddies! But still, something had to be said, and Jenny was glad that someone with as much clout as General McCarville was saying it.

General Power crouched down to one of his Bunker Hill campers. "What do you think about the alma, Isaac?"

"It's . . . good," Isaac said, hesitating.

"What about you, Owen?" he asked another.

"It's the best song ever, ever, ever!" Owen answered.

General Power shrugged at General McCarville. "Case in point."

"How convenient that you didn't ask the rest of the camp," she said. Jenny agreed. It being their first summer, the Bunker Hillers didn't know an alma from a march. They had no idea that the lyrics were supposed to conjure tears of pure camp joy.

"Do you want me to poll the rest of the team?" General Power asked. "Because I can poll every last—"

"Poll whoever you want," General McCarville cut in. "If we sing this, we will lose. These lyrics are an embarrassment to Rolling Hills. They're an anti-alma."

Jenny's heart skipped.

"An *anti-alma*?" he huffed.

"Where's the peace?" she asked. "Where's the love?"

Jenny looked around. The little Blue campers up front were wriggling. The ones in the middle were frozen. The older campers were sighing with frustration. The officers were whispering nervously. Jenny let her mind go as blank as paper. Then she channeled her angst into poetry, like she did at home, except this time the poetry was full of positive rhythms and rhymes. Forget "slaughter" and "yielding to power." The Blue alma mater needed "friends forever" and "groovy weather"! Lyrics that were inspirational! Moving! Creative! Ambitious! Bloated with peace and love! And most important, lyrics that fit this summer. Fit this war. Three-quarters back in the restless crowd, Jenny leapt to her feet and belted:

"Hey, Blue, you've done so well
When you fell you pushed on with spirit.
The Hatchet is not the heart of this war,
We're fighting for the people in it.

"And Rolling Hills, you make us feel so loved, so real
We carry our friends with us forever.
It's no surprise that as we grow we always know

That thinking of you brings groovy weather.
Nah nah nah nah nah, nah nah nah nah."

General Power's head flopped to the side. General McCarville's jaw dropped. The officers detangled themselves from their whisper-huddle. Everyone was gaping.

Jenny was mortified. What had she done? Had she just exposed her deep-seeded uncoolness to half the camp?! *Jenny Nolan isn't supposed to be a poet*, she thought. *She's supposed to be a . . .* She blinked, confused. *Cheerleader? Homecoming Queen? Miss Whatever?* That didn't feel right, either. She didn't know what she was supposed to be anymore.

And then a Sherri Hiller began a slow clap. The Highgate and Wawel Hillers joined in. Then the Notting, Faith, and Anita Hillers. Then the Hamburger, San Juan, and Jonah Hillers. Within thirty seconds, all of Blue was clapping, faster, faster, faster. A stampede of applause.

General Power surrendered with an *I don't know how to process this* shrug, and General McCarville took center stage. "Wow! Holy trippy wow!" As she gushed, the dark clouds finally crept over the court. "Jenny Nolan—those lyrics!" The clouds turned black. "Can you believe what that girl poured from her chords?" Before the camp could respond, the sky opened up and cried. Literally, a torrential downpour. Jenny's rendition had made Mother Earth feel all the warm and fuzzy feelings that the alma's first draft hadn't been able to.

"RUN FOR COVER!" General Power shouted.

The hills rumbled with thunder and the sky lit up in zigzags. Blue scattered.

Jenny dodged growing puddles and sprinted to the shelter of the Social Hall awning, where Sophie was standing and singing "Hare Krishna." Jenny assumed the song was some weird plea to the weather gods.

She felt someone behind her and spun around to find a soaked General McCarville. "Jenny," she pleaded, resting her blue-smudged forehead on Jenny's bangs. "You have to write it. Please. Write our alma mater. It's my last summer at the Hills and I need this victory."

Jenny's heart wanted to swell, but instead it ached. She hadn't been awarded Lieutenant for a reason. It had only taken her one egg murder, two heartbreaks, multiple friendship losses, and a double Hatchet travesty for that to ring clear. She'd be foolish to think SING would end any less terribly. As she'd decided yesterday, now was the time to lie low. To fade into the background. To leave Rolling Hills and never return. "I don't think it's a good idea," she finally said, breaking free.

"It's a very good idea," General McCarville argued. "C'mon. Those lyrics. You just—came up with them on the spot? That's insane!" She looked at Sophie. "Right? Tell her!"

"I prefer the term 'nutty as a fruitcake.' But yes, agreed."

Jenny sighed. How could she tell her General that if she let the team down one more time, she'd shame-spiral? That if she failed herself one more time, she'd never recover? "I just— I can't."

General McCarville nodded with understanding. She'd seen Jenny dig herself into a hole this week. "How about this," she began. "You write it. I'll pass it along to the Lieutenants as an anonymous submission. If they're on board, I'll say it was all you. If they veto it, you'll stay anonymous—no harm done."

Jenny mulled it over. She didn't want to disappoint her General by saying no. But she didn't want to say yes and then write something anti-alma-esque, something even more bitter than her poetry about Willamena and Christopher. After all, she wasn't feeling very mushy with love. Just because she was able to harness positivity for a couple of verses, didn't mean she had it in her to write a whole heartwarming song.

"She'll do it!" Sophie cried, hopping to Jenny's side.

"Um." Jenny bulged her eyes at Sophie, but General McCarville paid no mind. She was jumping up and down. "AMAZING! I haven't slept! I can't even string a coherent sentence together, let alone WRITE A WINNING ALMA MATER! Thank you, thank you, my BLESSED FLOWER CHILD!" And with that, she skipped away to her fellow officers.

Jenny turned to Sophie. "What was that?!"

"A chance to heal."

Jenny shook her head, trying to grasp what that meant. "Heal who? Me?" It's true writing poems made her feel better. She guessed Sophie understood that since she buried her head in books to make herself feel better, too. "What do you mean?"

"Yes, you. Lately you've been sadder than a hippie in a sports bra." She moved on before Jenny had a chance to question her metaphor. "If you really want to patch up your problems, write lyrics with a message. Let your words bring change! Revolution!"

Jenny's first thought was that Sophie was reading too much and socially interacting too little. But then again, maybe Sophie was on to something. Jenny had used every fiber of her being to hide all the uncool stuff about her. For four years. As someone who celebrated her uncoolness, could Sophie see right through Jenny's facade? Would her camp friends like her any less than they liked her now if she showed her true colors? "Hmmmm," Jenny mumbled while she sorted out the next steps. Maybe she could just be herself. Maybe she could try to write something totally heartwarming. Skies didn't just open up as she sang SING lyrics every day. Lightning didn't just strike when she wrote poetry at home. Sophie didn't just inspire her out of nowhere, or ever, really. Surely these were signs.

"All right, I'm in." Jenny rubbed her fingers together, wishing she had a pen in her hand. She had the sudden urge to write. This very instant.

Apparently, Sophie could tell, because she pushed Jenny out from under the awning and into the rain. "Go! Feel! Heal! Write!"

"Thanks, Sophster. Keep doing you," Jenny called over her shoulder, racing toward Faith Hill Cabin. The lightning flashed behind her. The hills shook with thunder. She stomped through puddles, and slipped through mudslides, and let the rain beat down on her head like a symphonic melody.

Three and a half hills later, Jenny arrived at her cabin a wheezing, muddy mess. She ran inside, pressed record on her contraband cell phone, rested it on the bathroom floor, and hopped into the shower. She hummed the alma melody over and over, asking herself what message she wanted to send and to who.

As Jenny watched the soap spiral into the drain at her flip-flopped feet, all of her camp memories rushed back to her like an end-of-summer slide show: Meeting Jamie for the first time and bonding over One Direction. Cuddle-spooning during thunderstorms, afraid their braces would get struck by lightning. Dancing together in matching sequined costumes four Campstocks in a row. Everything was once so magical.

The drain abruptly clogged with mud, and those same memories flashed through Jenny's mind in a totally unflattering light. She'd made fun of Jamie for saying Harry Styles was hottest. She'd told Jamie that their braces were likely to get struck by lightning so that Jamie wouldn't break the cuddle-spoon to play jacks with Missi. She'd never let Jamie help with the choreography in all of their Campstock history, even though Jamie had tried to help every summer.

Four years of ziplocked guilt vibrated inside her. She let the hot water run cold and the pressure go weak as she rehashed dozens of other favorite camp memories, now tainted with her power-hungry meanness. Their friendship had needed healing well before this war had even started.

Jenny shivered under the icy shower drizzle and sang a mournful song to Jamie about friendship and love and bonds meant to last a lifetime. It was honest and raw and simple and straight from her regretful heart. By the time she was done singing, her fingers had turned blue. She grabbed her pink towel from the curtain rod, wrapped herself, and stepped out of the shower. Standing there, with the celly in hand, was Melman.

"I can explain," Jenny said.

"Holy bologna, you genius." Melman took Jenny's hand and brought it to her wet cheek. "This is not from the rain."

"What is it from?" Jenny asked nervously.

"My eyes! My soul!"

Jenny laughed, and then, without warning, she began crying, too.

"Are you OK?" Melman asked.

"I don't know," Jenny sobbed. "I've been such a bad friend."

"Hey," Melman said. "Is this about Jamie?"

Jenny nodded through her tears. "I don't want to be a bad friend anymore. I turned Jamie into me. She wasn't mean before she met me. Everyone in this cabin was best friends, and I ruined it."

Melman led Jenny to Sophie's single bed. "Listen to me. You ruined nothing." They plopped down side by side. "Are you sometimes really annoying? Yes."

Jenny sputtered a laugh and then wiped her resurfacing tears.

"But we love you," Melman plowed on. "We love both of you. And at the end of the day, we're all best friends."

"You mean it? You're not just saying that because you're, like, the best Lieutenant ever?"

Melman gasped. "Did you just compliment me on my Lieutenantship?"

Jenny smiled. "I guess I did."

"Well, I think the new Jenny would be a kick-butt Lieutenant, too. This alma you wrote is off the charts. And Jamie needs to listen carefully. Because those lyrics are who we are. As a team and as a cabin." Melman rose with Jenny's cell phone and plucked a pen and paper from Sophie's stationery box. "We need to transcribe this STAT."

"And then what?" Jenny asked.

Melman looked at her funny. "Color War SING *her*story. It's about to be made, girl. And I've got your back."

August 13

Dear Brian,

Your mother and I see from the Hilltopper photos that Color War is under way and you are Lieutenant. Well done!

We wanted to let you know that Gramps is in the hospital, getting a hip replacement. His golf cart was rolling down the course toward a lagoon, and he tried to stop it superhero-style but fell old person-style. Good news: The golf cart did not drown. Bad news: Gramps's recovery is expected to be slow.

I haven't told him you're on Blue, but I'm sure he'll forgive you! We're so excited to see you keep the family tradition alive.

Love,

Pops

When the Deal Is Sealed

"Welcome, Blue and White, to the Sealed Envelope Ceremony!" the Captain megaphoned. She and TJ stood by the flagpole, surrounded by the entire camp. At their feet lay six Sealed Envelopes—three marked BLUE and three marked WHITE.

Play Dough's chest tightened with nerves. In mere minutes he'd know just how close he was to making his totally hip, metal-hipped Gramps proud.

TJ leaned into the megaphone. "It's hard to believe that today is the final day of Color War! The Captain and I have withheld the scores to let the suspense build." He paused dramatically. And then just as he opened his mouth to speak, he paused dramatically AGAIN. The camp roared with laughter. "Should we tell you now?"

The roars turned into screams. Some cheers broke out, like *"We want the scores! Hey! We want the scores!"* and *"Tell us now! Yeah! Tell us now!"*

The Captain laughed and quieted the crowd. "OK, then. TJ, take it away." She handed the megaphone over to her husband.

"What up, what up, what UP?" TJ asked, pointing to the sky. The morning's storm clouds had cleared, and the sky was now a balanced combo of clear blue and fluffy white. Blue cheered the historic cheer: *"The sky is blue, the lake is blue, we're gonna turn the White team blue!"* White overlapped: *"The clouds are white, Hill Hall is white, we're gonna turn the Blue team white!"*

"Yes, nature supports all colors," TJ mused. "Sports 'n' spirit points, here we go." The camp fell into a thigh-clapping drum-roll and stopped short on TJ's fist-clenched cue. "Blue has a score of 679, and White has a 52-point lead with a score of 731!"

White rose to their feet, high-fiving, fist-pumping, hooting and hollering. Blue clapped weakly. Play Dough tried not to let his stomach flip with worry. His team might have been behind, but the Sealed Envelopes were still sealed. Surely the Rope Burn was worth enough points to surpass White's lead. Last summer it had been worth 150 points. The summer before that: 125. The summer before that: 175. He bet this summer it was worth 200!

"And now, for the Sealed Envelopes!" TJ barreled on. "Can the Hamburger and Faith Hill Lieutenants please make their way to the flagpole?"

Play Dough swallowed hard and rose from his knees to meet Melman by the Blue-marked envelopes. Totle and Jamie made their way to the White-marked ones. TJ greeted each of the campers with a pound. "Choose your envelopes. Blue, you'll open yours first."

"Which one should we open?" Play Dough whispered to Melman.

She pointed to the one in the middle. "I think maybe that one?"

"OK." Play Dough was on board for whatever. As long as the points were high and he got to enjoy the rush of Blue celebration. He bent down to the Sealed Envelope and tore it open. Inside was an index card. He and Melman looked at it together. It said ROPE BURN. Play Dough grinned and flipped it over to find out its worth. His heart did a swan dive.

"Well?" TJ prompted.

Play Dough looked at Melman, who was looking back at him, frozen in horror. "I think it's a mistake," he told TJ.

TJ shook his head. "Nope. Whatever's writ is legit! And remember, the envelopes are sealed before the war begins—nothing's rigged. The Captain and I just like to keep you all on your toes." He passed Play Dough the megaphone while the camp grumbled with anticipation.

"Rope Burn is worth twenty points." Play Dough dropped the megaphone to his side and let it hang there limply. After a few seconds of silent shock, Blue erupted into a cacophony of boos and hisses. They weren't directed at him—it wasn't his fault that the Rope Burn was worth so little—but that didn't make him feel any less crappy. All of his blood, sweat, tears, and face paint had gone into making that fire. And for what? The same amount of points they could earn for a spick-and-span cabin? The same amount of points the Bunker Hillers could earn for winning a game of newcomb? This was criminal! And insane! This meant that Rope Burn wasn't his big comeback after all! He was still the epic failure he was three days ago.

Melman pried the megaphone from Play Dough's fingers and passed it back to TJ. "And now, White!" TJ exclaimed.

Totle and Jamie opened their envelope. "Tug-o-War," they said together, "is worth ninety points!"

White cheered: *"WE P-U-L-L, PULLED THE ROPE!"*

Play Dough's heart buried itself in some neighboring organ. Last summer, Tug-o-War had been worth forty points. The summer before that: thirty-five points. Ninety points was unheard of! What was going on?

"Don't worry," Melman whispered. "Maybe the Bucket Brigade and Apache will be worth more than we think."

"Maybe," Play Dough said, trying not to melt down in front of the whole camp.

"Thank you, Hamburger and Faith Hill Lieutenants," TJ megaphoned. "Next up to do the honors are the Wawel and Notting Hill Lieutenants!"

Play Dough sulked back into the crowd and held his breath as White Lieutenants Wagner and Kreitzer peeled open the next envelope. They broke into enormous smiles. "Color Bowl—holy moly!—it's worth a whopping 115 points!" Kreitzer cried.

White celebrated with a chant: *"Don't start with us! We're smart like us! We put the 'triv' in 'trivia'!"*

Play Dough exhaled with misery. For a team that called themselves smart, their chant made zero sense. It was actually the dumbest chant he'd ever heard. He told himself to let it go and refocused on Blue, now opening their envelope. "Please, please, please let us earn the points back," he mumbled to himself. "We can still do this."

Lieutenant Shale reported, deadpan: "Bucket Brigade is worth sixty-five points."

Play Dough shook with rage. Sixty-five points? The Bucket

Brigade was normally worth at least a hundred! He tried to think about happy stuff like turkey gravy sandwiches and Chunky Monkey ice cream to settle his nerves, but that quickly led him to think about his Gramps, who loved a good binge eat, too. This very moment, his favorite family member was at some smelly, boring hospital in Boca Raton with nothing to distract him from his suffering but the hope that his grandson was following in his footsteps. Play Dough had come so far. He'd worked so hard. He couldn't disappoint his Gramps now. Blue had to win. They had to!

The cheering and booing settled as the Highgate and Sherri Hill Lieutenants opened the last of the Sealed Envelopes. Play Dough's stomach knotted up like a pretzel.

"Apache Relay," Blue Lieutenants Saad and Figg announced. "One hundred points."

"Novelty Relays," White Lieutenants Burrick and Kasnett announced. "One hundred and seventy-five points."

Play Dough groaned.

TJ took back the megaphone and slipped an envelope from his pocket. "And just for fun, had the Hatchet not suffered an attempted drowning, it would have been worth . . ." Play Dough didn't want to know. He bet it was worth a ton. At least 200 points, maybe 225. That would be just his luck. ". . . 330 points! What's sealed has been revealed!"

NOOOOOOOOO! Play Dough felt like he was being smothered to death by asparagus, his least favorite vegetable. He buried his face in the crook of his elbow and bit his tongue to keep from shouting. Not that his shouting would have caused a scene. Blue was rumbling with disappointment, and White was belting praises to the Color War Gods. It was mayhem.

"All right, all right, settle down," the Captain demanded. "Please be patient with us while we recalculate the scores."

Play Dough lifted his face just enough to watch Steinberg sprint to the megaphone. "864—Blue. 1,111—WHIIIIIITE!"

The Captain looked down at the numbers and nodded affirmatively. "Correct! Thank you, Robert Steinberg. White is ahead by 247 points."

Play Dough peered through the chaos and spotted Jenny. She was rebraiding one of her pigtails, totally unbothered. How? He caught her eye, and before he could embarrassingly look away, she mouthed at him: "The war's not over until the hippie team sings."

It took a couple seconds to set in, but eventually Play Dough felt the smallest pinch of relief. With SING in two hours and worth five hundred points, this war was still up for grabs. "So let's sing," he mouthed back.

Lieutenant Nederbauer,

Whassup? Tonight is the night—break legs!

From one officer to another, I encourage you to listen to the Blue alma. Jenny wrote it, totally inspired by your friendship. She misses you and wants to start fresh.

Give her another shot? Do it for Faith.

Let's make memories,
Lieutenant Melman

COLOR WAR SING

Entrance and Costume. 25 points.

Dance. 100 points.

Plaque. 25 points.

Scenery. 50 points.

March. 150 points.

Alma Mater. 150 points.

The judges split points between Blue and White for each SING category.

SING! It's starting! Omigod, omigod! **Through one of its** windows, Jenny peered into the Social Hall for the first time since the war had started and was totally overwhelmed by its transformation. White Awesome Eighties had taken over the front of the hall. Onstage was a pyramid of cardboard boxes painted with the MTV logo. Above the pyramid hung a Madonna poster. A Jane Fonda workout was projected stage left and a Richard Simmons workout was projected stage right. A Rubik's Cube dangled from the ceiling like a disco ball. Neon was everywhere.

Even the campers were costumed to the theme: The Bunker and One Tree Hillers were Muppet Babies; the Tyler and Two Tree Hillers were Teenage Mutant Ninja Turtles; the Jonah and Lauryn Hillers were the Smurfs; the San Juan and Anita Hillers were Pac-Men; the Hamburger Hillers sported mullet wigs; the Faith Hillers wore off-the-shoulder sweatshirts and leggings; the Wawel Hillers were Beetlejuices; the Notting Hillers were the DuckTales; and lastly, the Highgate and Sherri Hillers sported aviator glasses, acid-washed jeans, and Members Only jackets. Their entrance music: Madonna's "Like a

Prayer," which everyone was obviously belting their faces off to, including the judges.

White's set was so awesome-sauce, Jenny was nervous to look at her team's half of the hall. But she was shocked and relieved to find that Blue's was even better. Trippy, psychedelic lights were projected onto the black-papered walls. Beaded curtains hung over the back entrance. Human-size lava lamps stood in the corners. Big mushroom piñatas hung from the ceiling. The floors were littered with tie-dyed pillows and paisley rugs. A retired golf cart was decked out like a hippie mobile, draped in flowers and painted with declarations like LAY, DON'T SLAY and HECK NO, WE WON'T GO! A fog machine made everything kind of hazy—like the Social Hall was on some far-off planet!

"Like a Prayer" cut out and the Beach Boys' "Good Vibrations" took its place. Jenny watched with glee as Blue's Lower Camp skipped in as flower children—barefoot with flowing pants and skirts, and flowers woven into their braided hair. Middle Camp entered next as Grateful Dead fans (aka Deadheads), dressed head to toe in tie-dye. Upper Camp entered last, decked out fabulously in bell-bottoms, suede vests, and beaded necklaces. *Holy hippie perfection*, Jenny thought. *It's already a night to remember!*

Buzzing with anticipation, she left the window to join the dozen Blue team dancers stretching on the grass. They wore matching white flowy dresses with baby's breath in their hair, and with the sun setting behind them, the whole scene looked as whimsical as an Urban Outfitters ad. From inside the Social Hall, Jenny could hear the Captain delivering her "Welcome to Color War SING" speech, outlining what was to come—the team dances, the plaque exhibition, the Generals' entrances, the marches, and, last but not least, the alma maters.

Just hearing the term "alma mater" made the hair on the back of Jenny's neck go prickly. She was so nervous-slash-excited. She wanted to get to her songwriting debut as quickly as possible while also making every moment of SING last. It had always been her favorite night of the summer, and not even the drama of this Color War could change that.

"Are you ladies ready?" Lieutenant Figg asked, coming out of a backbend. She'd choreographed Blue team's dance and was performing as well, which was an honor, considering she was the best gymnast in all of Rolling Hills and also maybe Westchester.

"Just a sec," one of the Sherri Hillers said, mussing up her banana curls. Some others adjusted their footless tights. Jenny felt her dress pocket, where she'd tucked her apology letter to Play Dough and a revised apology letter to Jamie. If the alma mater didn't win Jamie over, at least the letter might. As for Play Dough, Jenny had no grand plan. She noticed how sad he'd looked at the Sealed Envelope Ceremony and figured it might cheer him up to know someone still believed in him. But how she'd deliver the letter to him without it being super-awkward and a déjà vu of his rejection was unclear. More likely than not, his letter would live and die in her dress pocket. *Negative yay.*

Jenny and her codancers grabbed hands, and in a line chasséd along the perimeter of the Social Hall to the back doors. "Is your heart pounding as loud as mine is?" Jenny asked Lieutenant Finkelstein, who was the dancer in front of her.

Lieutenant Finkelstein sighed a yes. "We've just got to feel the flow."

"Totally," Jenny said.

Just then, Lieutenant Figg cued DJ Steinberg with a peace sign. Steinberg brought his headphones up over his ears and pressed play. The *Hair* medley began with "Aquarius."

Jenny's stomach fluttered with nerves as she skipped through the beaded curtain, hurried past the Upper Camp hippies, the Middle Camp Deadheads, and the Lower Camp flower children and formed a circle with her codancers in the center of the Social Hall. The horns swelled, and Jenny let herself fall into a trance of body bending and waving. She didn't care what she looked like or who was watching—her spirit was one with the music, and that was all that mattered!

Lieutenant Figg launched the next song—"Hair"—with two perfect back handsprings. Jenny began jumping up and down, throwing her hair around, and dancing out the week's hurt and anger. It felt so therapeutic! She considered incorporating this kind of dance into her relationship therapy—that is, if being a relationship therapist was still in the cards. She guessed she'd have more clarity by the end of the night.

"Let the Sunshine In" rang out last, and Jenny and her team pulled the other Lieutenants and even judges (Claudia Cooking, Bill Tennis, Mark Waterski, Rick, and Sara) into their spirited mosh pit of love. By the final chorus, everyone was bursting with newfound hope and joy.

Totally winded and high on life, Jenny took a seat up front while White's music kicked in: Michael Jackson's "Thriller." She watched the crowd go wild for Lieutenant Kasnett, a zombie in a poufy party dress, as she led a team of twenty zombie boys and girls in the "Thriller" choreography. It was P-E-R-F-E-C-T. But the most amazing part was Jamie. She was dressed like Michael Jackson's girlfriend in the music video—orange heels, gray-blue leopard-print leggings, an orange T-shirt under a jean jacket, orange stud earrings, and a weird curly mullet. She ran from her supernatural dance team, doing pirouettes and screaming. It was the performance of a lifetime, and Jenny was so giggly and proud of her BFF, she had tears welling up in her eyes.

The music ended, and Jenny joined Blue in a standing ovation. She watched the judges note Blue's über-sportsmanship and White's über-spirit and scribble feverishly onto their SING rubric. Both teams were so unique and amazing! How could the judges possibly choose one winner?

"And now for the plaques!" the Captain announced. "Will the Blue and White artists please bring their work forward?"

Slimey and a Blue Notting Hiller entered from the side doors, holding their plaques. They went up and down the aisles and then did a lap in the center, at which point Jenny saw just how cool their designs were. White's plaque was painted neon orange and titled I ♥ WHITE AWESOME '80S. Underneath the title was an old-school boom box with GENERAL SILVER painted inside the left speaker and GENERAL FERRARA painted inside the right. Below that was a stack of six cassette tapes, each labeled with a different Lieutenant's name. As a smiling Slimey passed by, Jenny chimed in to the chorus of compliments.

Of course, Jenny complimented the Notting Hill artist, too. Blue's plaque had colors that seemed to jump off the wood. Under BLUE PSYCHEDELIC '60S was a flower-crowned hippie sporting round purple-tinted sunglasses. Painted inside the left lens was GENERAL POWER and inside the right was GENERAL MCCARVILLE. In the background were spiraling rainbows. Inside of each colored band were the Lieutenants' names in bubble letters. To top it off, the plaque was bordered with pressed flowers. After their walking tours, the artists rested their artwork on the judges' table and joined their teams.

"Wow," the Captain said. "The plaques are stunning. They'll be a wonderful addition to the Dining Hall." Through the applause, it hit Jenny that she wouldn't have her name on the wall like she'd once dreamed, and that stung. But then she reminded herself that there were more important things at stake than her bubbly name in a spiral. And, hey, she was only a Faith Hiller—she had time to leave a legacy if that was what she truly wanted.

Next, the Captain brought the Highgate and Sherri Hill Lieutenants up to the stage to announce the Generals' entrances. General Silver entered as Michael Jackson in a hot-orange jacket and tight orange jeans. He broke through the MTV pyramid and moonwalked across the stage. General Ferrara entered as Madonna in a hot-pink ball gown and fake diamonds. She was carried in by six tuxedoed counselors à la the "Material Girl" music video. General Power made his entrance to "Purple Haze," costumed as Jimi Hendrix, bare-chested with an open velvet jacket and a red bandana in his ’fro wig. General McCarville came in swinging from one of the mushroom piñatas, costumed as Janis Joplin in a short, sleeveless gold dress with round pink-tinted sunglasses.

As both teams continued to go ballistic, the Generals huddled in the center of the Social Hall for the coin toss to determine the song order. Jenny crossed her fingers that the Blue alma would be last so she could find Jamie right after, the words still ringing in the air. The Captain announced the results: “First up for the march: Blue. First up for the alma mater: White.” *Score-sauce!* Jenny uncrossed her fingers with a huge smile.

General McCarville and General Power climbed on top of their chairs, their arms out toward their team, ready to conduct. Jenny perked up. TJ cued Steinberg with a thumbs-up, and he played the Foundations’ 1968 hit “Build Me Up Buttercup.” Alongside her team, Jenny leapt to her feet and sang:

“*Tune into Woodstock now (Woodstock now),*
holy wow, Blue team
Just a groovy sound (groovy sound),
the Beatles break ground
And the funk of it (funk of it), you never sit, Blue team
There’s no time for that (time for that),
you better dance STAT
Listen up, listen up, Jimi Hendrix is playin’
You know it’s the summer of love
So tune on in (tune on in), watch out White, Blue soars above”

By the last chorus, everyone in the Social Hall was clapping. Blue belted out the last line: *"So tune on in (tune on in), Psychedelic Sixties has won!"* Even though Blue didn't actually know if they'd won the march and were far behind in the grand scheme of the war, the team sang with such passion that it was hard to believe they wouldn't be taking home all the wins. Jenny hugged random One Tree Hillers around her even though she didn't know their names, and then sat down to watch White.

Steinberg played Katrina and the Waves' 1983 song "Walking on Sunshine." Jenny noted that the lyrics didn't fit the music as well as Blue's, but the chorus was really catchy:

"We're playing Nintendo (whoa oh)
The Rubik's Cube—nailed it (whoa oh)
Let's go Dirty Dancing (whoa oh)
The Awesome Eighties (HEY!)
All right now
The Awesome Eighties (HEY!)"

When they finished, Jenny assessed: White's march was pretty good; Blue's was way better. The White team stayed standing for their alma, which was to Cyndi Lauper's 1986 release "True Colors." From the first lyric, it was moving: *"Hearts beating quickly, seeing new faces stepping off the bus."* It brought Jenny back to that very first bus ride to camp, where her friendship with Jamie had begun. Then her mind skipped from memory to memory: the way she and Jamie shared Creamsicles;

the time Jenny braided Jamie's hair into her own so they'd be attached at the head for the day; the time Jamie was sick in the infirmary, so Jenny pretended she was, too, just so they could be together. Now Jenny looked at Jamie singing the chorus and tried not to cry.

"Our summer home where friendships
Grow so strong
From different places
Yet we come together.
United we stand, supporting each other
Mile wide smiles
Uncontrolled giggles
Bonds beautiful as a rainbow."

Jenny caught Jamie's eye on the last line of the chorus, and Jenny lost it. The tears slipped down her burning cheeks. Jamie's face went into pre-cry mode, lip-biting and all. Did that mean Jamie was ready to forgive her? Or was she just emotional from the song? When White finished, Jenny gave them a standing ovation. She could feel her team eyeing her like she was possessed by the magic of SING, which she probably was, but whatever. This was for Jamie.

White sat down, so Jenny sat, too. General McCarville rose onto one of the chairs. *Alma time!* In her head, Jenny ran through the opening to the Blue alma mater. She tried to imagine what Jamie's face would look like if the memories rushed back to her as they had to Jenny in the shower.

"Jenny? Is Jenny Nolan in the house?"

Jenny whipped her attention to General McCarville. Her heart began to race. She rose with hesitation. "Yeah?"

General McCarville pointed to the empty chair beside her. "You're conducting with me, girl." Jenny let the words echo in her head before she was able to fully understand them. *Conduct? With her?* When the meaning hit, she could hardly breathe, she was so overwhelmed and excited. Conducting was one of the biggest honors in all of camp. No camper, not even the one who had grown up to be a real-live conductor, had ever conducted in Rolling Hills history. It was reserved for the Generals and the Generals only. What was happening?!

She looked over at General Power basking in the trippy lights. He gave her a "go ahead" nod. Her eyes wandered to a sexy Play Dough in a dreadlocked wig, bell-bottoms that were six inches too long, and a white fringed shirt. He gave Jenny a thumbs-up that knocked the nerves right out of her.

As Jenny made her way to the chair, she looked back at Jamie. "This is for you," she mouthed. Jenny stepped up beside General McCarville. She wiped her face dry and looked out at the 150 sets of eyes focused on her.

As the "Hey Jude" intro swelled, Jenny realized that, facing her team, she wasn't going to be able to sing to Jamie. She wasn't going to be able to track Jamie's emotions or gauge her forgiveness. But that was OK, she told herself. She didn't want to stifle her best friend. All Jenny needed to do was conduct her team and trust that the message would hit Jamie as hard as White's alma had hit her.

"Hey, you, I miss your smile,
Been a while since I wrote a letter
The mem'ries live inside of my heart
And then they restart and everything's better"

Jenny's left leg began shaking. She couldn't tell if she was uneasy conducting, or worried that the judges wouldn't like her song, or terrified that Jamie wouldn't relate, or all three. *Keep it together*, she pleaded.

"Hey, White, although we fight
Our friendship cannot be broken
Remember the cuddle-spoons that we've shared
No war can tear the bonds we have woven"

Now her face was damp. Sweat? Tears? Probably both. She wanted to wipe it, but her arms were busy conducting. The wetness amplified as her arms waved around to the beat. She felt crazy and overheated—was she having early onset hot flashes? Her grammy once told her they ran in the family.

"So hug it out and let me in, hey friend, we win
Regatta a lotta stars to thank tonight
The winter's long but summer's strong, hey friend, this song
Will carry you through ten months for just two
Nah nah nah nah nah, nah nah nah nah, yeah"

Her team had their arms slung over each other's shoulders, swaying to the beat. Normally swaying was cheesy and distracting, because everyone moved in different directions, but not this time. Blue was totally in sync.

Jenny suddenly got the urge to be bold. She looked at General McCarville. She was doing great. She looked back at her team. They were doing great. It was time to check on Jamie. She hopped off the chair, walked toward her best friend, and sang the last verse directly to her.

"Hey, you, I see your smile
Been a while since I got your letter
The mem'ries soar inside of my heart
Now they'll restart and make it better"

As the music faded, Jenny could hear the entire camp sobbing. She imagined that, if her home friends were here, they'd think every endangered species had just gone extinct. She'd have a hard time explaining that, no, it's just that everyone's obsessed with camp and didn't want it to end in two days. Jenny let the emotional chaos fade to white noise and took in Jamie's glassy eyes. They looked like melting Hershey's Kisses.

Jenny held the letter out to Jamie, and she hesitantly took it. "Jamie. Before you read this, I just want to say three things."

Jamie nodded an OK.

"One: You were so brilliant tonight, and you were brilliant

all week as Lieutenant, and you've always been brilliant, and I should have given you room to shine a long time ago."

The residual anger in Jamie's eyes washed away, and Jenny could feel their psychic-squad connection come alive. Jamie was giving Jenny access to her mind, and the message was loud and clear: *I miss you, Jenny. I want to play jacks with you and dance with you and have everything go back to the way it was, only better.*

Jenny knew she could respond to Jamie in her mind, but she didn't want their revived friendship to be a secret. So she carried on with her list. "Two: I miss you so much it hurts."

Jamie's hands, which were in little fists, began to uncurl.

"When I wrote the alma I realized how much I treasure our friendship and how I would do anything to win you back. Jamie Lynn Nederbauer, you are my Bestest Best Friend."

"What's the third thing?" Jamie asked.

"I'm sorry. Like truly, truly, for-real sorry."

Jamie smiled weakly, and then the tears started streaming down her face. "I'm sorry I called you a cheater."

"It's OK," Jenny said. "I did cheat."

"I've been excluding you and only hanging out with Missi."

Jenny shrugged. "Sometimes I watch the two of you and I'm like *Wow, they've got a really good friendship, too,* and I think that makes me really jealous because we're best friends," Jenny admitted. "But what if the three of us were besties?"

"That would be nice."

"Miss Jen-Jam."

Jamie laughed. "You're so genius at mash-up names!"

For a brief moment, they took in the rest of the camp. Everyone seemed to be hugging it out, a mosh pit of Blue and White love. Blite love.

"I'm so sorry about Christopher," Jamie blurted. "Play Dough told me. I should've been there for you. I should've told myself, 'It's a Christopher crisis and Jenny needs me,' or, like, 'It's a J-squad crisis and we need each other.'"

Jenny shook her head. "Christopher's a jerk. There's a bigger fish in the sea."

"Do you mean plenty of fish?"

Play Dough passed by behind Jamie, and Jenny felt her heart flutter-kick at twice its normal rate. Was it possible that his rejection just made her like him more? Or did she just like him so much that she didn't care if the feeling was mutual? Jenny searched her mind for an analogy and thought about *Beauty and the Beast*. It was almost like Play Dough was a beast and she was a beauty, except on the inside he was a beauty and she was . . . well, she was also beautiful on the inside now. And she dug Play Dough's outer beauty, too, even if everyone else was blind to it. *Wow, my life really is like a Disney movie,* Jenny thought. Except without the happily ever after.

Jenny finally broke her gaze to look at Jamie, who was gaping at her. Jamie glanced over her shoulder and then back at Jenny. "Omigod, you were staring at Play Dough!"

"Omigod, no!" *There is no way I was that obvious,* Jenny thought.

"Omigod, yes, you were! And this letter"—Jamie waved it in

the air—"tells me exactly how you feel about him."

Jenny froze. "Wait."

Jamie began to read the letter aloud: "Dear Play Dough, Sometimes love finds you on the lake at midnight. We're not the likeliest pair. But when I'm with you—"

Jenny snatched the paper from Jamie's hand. "That's the wrong letter."

"You think?!" Jamie asked. "So, you really like him?"

"I do," Jenny admitted. "I kissed him on the trambopoline. Is that 'ew'?"

"JENNY!" Jamie squealed with joy. "If you actually like him, then he's not 'ew.' He's hot tamales. Smooching on the trambopoline? That's so romantic."

Jenny grinned. "I thought so, too." She was aching for a Jamie hug. How had she survived this week without her best friend? She needed to double confirm this fight was over. "So . . . ," she said.

"So . . . ," Jamie followed.

"Are you still mad at me?" Jenny asked, crossing her fingers behind her back.

"No way. Like you wrote in the alma, 'Our friendship cannot be broken.'"

Jenny uncrossed with relief.

"She-FFs are BFFs!" they squealed together. "Jinx! Double jinx! Triple jinx! Quadruple jinx! What does She-FFs even mean? Omigod, I've missed you." Jamie and Jenny stared into each other's eyes, at a loss for more overlapping words, and then embraced.

"Play Dough was right. I should have made up with you a long time ago." Jamie gasped. "Uh-oh." She pulled away, and Jenny watched as the color in her face drained from caramel to manila-folder beige.

"What's wrong?"

"You're gonna hate me. I'm scared."

"I could never hate you." Jenny held Jamie's cheeks. "The only thing I hate about you is not being friends with you."

"OK, well, I may have, out of really big anger and jealousy, told Play Dough you were using him and that he shouldn't be your puppet."

"When?"

"At Rope Burn. Please don't be mad!"

So that's *why Play Dough rejected me at the Regatta!* Jenny realized. They'd shared this magical moment of love, and then Jamie had stomped on his hopes and dreams. Jenny wasn't his PR nightmare. Play Dough just had to learn that Jenny thought he was amazing and would never hurt him again, and then they could share kisses and happiness and a camp wedding and a honeymoon in Hawaii and three teacup maltipoos and the nickname "Dough Jenny."

"Jenny!" Jamie waved a hand in front of Jenny's face. "You're smiling. Why are you smiling? Say something, you're scaring me!"

"I didn't like Play Dough like that at first, Jamie, and I did use him to get you in trouble—it's not like you lied. But I'm a woman now, and my feelings have changed. Play Dough's only upset with me because he has no idea where I am emotionally."

“Where are you emotionally?”

“I’m here.” She pulled Jamie’s hand over her heart.

Missi was lurking a few feet away, clearly jealous of their reunion. “Missi, get your butt over here,” Jenny demanded. Missi scampered over, and Jenny let her feel her heart, too. Now that Jenny knew how sucky it felt to be left out, it was the least she could do. Plus, Missi wasn’t so bad. She was only half as mean as Jenny was to her, and Jenny couldn’t blame her for wanting a taste of popularity. It tasted good. But it wasn’t everything.

“It’s beating really fast,” Missi said.

“Sometimes fate just, like, happens,” said Jamie.

Jenny sighed. “At some point, you have to stop planning it and just live your life.”

“Totally,” Missi and Jamie said together.

“Wait, so are we all friends again?” Missi asked.

Jenny deferred to Jamie with a smile.

“You know it,” Jamie said. “We’re Miss Jen-Jam.”

“Ooooh!” Missi said. “I like it!”

Jamie snatched back Play Dough’s letter and slipped out of the huddle. “I gotta get this in the right hands,” she said. Before Jenny could protest, or Missi could voice her confusion, Jamie shuffled off in her “Thriller” heels.

The Captain interrupted with an announcement. “Blue and White, we’ve calculated the SING scores and, well . . .” Even though they were on opposing teams, Jenny and Missi squeezed hands like they were in this together. “We’re in an unprecedented pickle: Color War is tied.”

FLASH APACHE RELAY

A series of events tied together with a baton handoff.

1. **Archery.** Must get bull's-eye.
2. **Tennis Ball Bouncing.** One hundred consecutive bounces, no mess-ups.
3. **Tennis Ball Sweep.** Using a broom, weave through orange cones.
4. **Rollerblading.** Around perimeter of the court.
5. **Backward Foul Shot.** Get it in. Not facing the hoop.
6. **Chocolate Bar Ingestion.** Swallow it.
7. **Color Bowl.** Camp Rolling Hills trivia.

RULES

The first team that finishes wins it all.

Making Your Mark

Play Dough took a deep breath and flipped over the final index card from the judges' table. Up top it read ANCHOR and below that, CAMP TRIVIA.

"That's it, folks," TJ announced. "The winner of this summer's Color War will depend on a first-ever tiebreaker: a flash Apache Relay. We've got seven events for the officers. First team to complete the relay wins!"

Play Dough swallowed and tried to digest the magnitude of what was to come. He and Melman were going to be the last leg. The Apache Relay would come down to them and their brainpower. The stakes? Oh, just the highest they'd ever been. He peeled off his wig and shook his head, his sweat flying in all directions.

Melman put a hand on his shoulder. "Dude, you OK?"

"Uhhhh."

"You're acting like a wet dog."

"Are you good at camp trivia?" he blurted.

"Eh. Better at sports," Melman said. "Wish I were doing the backward foul shot."

"Yeah, and I'm way more suited for the chocolate bar event. I can eat an entire Hershey's bar in six seconds."

"Eek. I doubt Lieutenant Shale can do it that fast."

"I know. And he's basically a camp encyclopedia. He should be doing the trivia. We should switch!" Play Dough lunged forward. "HEY, SHALE!"

Melman gripped Play Dough's shoulders and pulled him back. "PD, you know there's no switching. Pull yourself together. You're gonna be great. *We're* gonna be great."

Play Dough nodded, but he wasn't so sure. He got time and a half on tests in school. Could he ask for that now? Why hadn't he been born with Steinberg's brain? Or Dover's? Why had his mom declared that his Ritalin was only for the school year?! He really wished his Gramps' recovery wasn't riding on him. That his team wasn't riding on him.

"Oh, I forgot about . . ." Melman pulled a piece of pink stationery from her bell-bottom butt pocket. "This is from Jamie."

Play Dough narrowed his eyes. "Why did Jamie write me a letter?"

"I have no idea," she admitted. "She was blabbing on about how everything she'd told you about Jenny was a lie, but I wasn't really paying attention, 'cause, like, you know, we're at the peak of war."

Play Dough took it, his heart slamming. He may have been mad at Jenny, but after crushing on her for four summers, and then kissing and falling in love with her, he didn't have much control over his body. He unfolded it and read to himself.

Dear Play Dough,
Sometimes love finds you on the lake at midnight. We're not the likeliest pair. But when I'm with you I don't care what anyone else thinks. You're the sloppy joe to my gluten-free bread. The loud mouth to my proud mouth. The fart to my art. Will you be the TJ to my Captain, aka my BF? I'm lucky to have fallen for a guy like you.
xo, Jenny

He could feel his face turn beet red. Tomato red. Strawberry red. All the reds. He looked up at Melman. "You're right. We're gonna do great."

Melman laughed. "Wow, Jamie really knows how to inspire her opponents."

"You could say that." Play Dough scanned the crowd for Jenny and spotted her beside Sophie, chanting for Blue. She spotted him—pomegranate-faced and gaping, with the letter in his hand. She grinned the most beautiful grin. He nearly melted.

"What's happening?" Melman asked, snapping him back. "You look like you've been punched in the face."

"With love."

"Excuse me?"

General Power was suddenly between them. "I need one of you to stay back while the rest of the officers set up the Apache on the basketball court."

Play Dough shot his hand up. "I got it." He was juggling so many emotions, he could use some rallying time with the team. And Jenny, specifically.

"I was hoping you'd volunteer," General Power said. "Melman actually understands sports equipment."

"I agree," Play Dough declared, smiling ear to ear. He wasn't dumb—he'd registered the dig. He was just so elated about Jenny and so terrified about the upcoming trivia to get bogged down by General Power's insults. Play Dough knew his own strengths. He knew what he was capable of. He knew when life was full of possibility!

General Power raised his eyebrows curiously. Melman shrugged. Then they headed toward the back doors. "See ya in a bit, PD," Melman called over her shoulder.

"Yup." Play Dough grabbed a wireless mic and tapped it twice. Then he threw his fingers into a peace sign and swept the peace sign across his forehead. *"Yodel, yodel, yodel, yodel, yodel, yodel-oo!"*

Blue shouted back with the same peace sign move. *"Yodel, yodel, yodel, yodel, yodel, yodel-oo!"*

Play Dough chanted: *"Groovy, hippie, Psychedelic Blue!"* It was followed by complete silence. Blue had gotten good at getting quiet on demand. "In just a few minutes, we are going to compete in the most intense Apache Relay there ever was. That aside, I want to say thank you. Thank you, Blue, for letting me lead you and for reminding me what this war is all about. Tonight's alma mater stole our hearts, which is the only kind of stealing that's moral." He shoved the mic under his armpit and gave a double thumbs-up. "To quote Jenny Nolan: 'You've done so well. When you fell, you pushed on with spirit. The Hatchet is not the heart of this war.'" Play Dough pointed the mic out to the crowd.

They sang back: *"We're fighting for the people in it!"*

"Inspiration-sauce! As for the rest of the song, I don't know what 'cuddle-spooning' is, but if there's food on a spoon, I'm down with cuddling, too."

Blue chuckled. Dover yelled out, "Play Dough's the man!" and someone else yelled, "Cuddle-spooning's cool!" He imagined that made Jenny feel good, so that made him feel good, too.

"Also, if I'm tripping up or making no sense, blame it on the 'shrooms." He pointed to the mushroom piñatas. "I inhaled a lot of paint today while decorating them, which is making them look even more psychedelic, which, BT dubs, has nothing to do with deli sandwiches."

Blue got hysterical.

"So, yeah, us officers are going to pour all we've got into this tiebreaker. But remember, Blue team, no matter the outcome, we've already made camp history."

Play Dough dropped the mic and the crowd went wild. *"GO DOUGH OR GO HOME!"* morphed into *"FEEL THE DOUGH!"* which then morphed into *"LET THE DOUGH RISE!"*

Through the window, Play Dough saw General Power jogging back from the basketball court, his face creased with annoyance. He hustled inside, stepped in front of Play Dough, and waved his arms to quiet his team. Nothing. He tried the peace sign move and the yodeling. Nothing. Play Dough offered the mic, but he slapped it away. The chanting had gotten so chaotic, General Power had to stand on a chair and blow his whistle three times to get noticed. Play Dough left the mic by General Power's feet, just in case he changed his mind, and once Blue finally hushed, the General bent down and grabbed it.

"Glad to see the high energy, Blue, but all I asked of Lieutenant Garfink was to stay back with you. Not make an Academy Award speech to the whole camp over the mic." There was some laughter, but it was mostly awkward. General Power shook his head anxiously. "In the army he'd get chewed out for this." There was no laughter; it was entirely awkward. This was not how either of them deserved to go out.

Play Dough tried to pluck the mic from General Power's hand, but General Power held it tight, like a greedy toddler.

"May I, General?" Play Dough asked as politely as he could, which made him sound British. Some kids up front giggled.

General Power dropped his eyes and surrendered. "Sure," he said. "Do whatever clown act you want."

Play Dough thought about correcting him and saying "stand-up," but he knew better. He also thought about honking General Power's nose. But he knew better than to do that, too. He took the high road. "Thanks," he said and then faced Blue. "So, before I take my place on the court, I want to give one final shout-out to the face of the war, the man who's been leading tirelessly this week with precision and decision and cognition and ambition and volition." Play Dough did not know what four-fifths of those words meant, but he knew they rhymed and so that was good. "Stand up and go crazy for my hero and your one-and-only GEN-ER-AL POWEEERRRR!"

Blue cheered like mad. Play Dough rubber-snake danced through the crowd, chanting: *"POWER'S GOT POWER, SO WE'VE GOT POWER!"* As the cheering grew louder and the hype got hyper, Play Dough looked back at General Power in the center of the hall. He was rubber-snake dancing, too. Play Dough handed him the mic, and this time he took it, with something unrecognizable on his face. It was a smile. *Huh.*

Play Dough strode to his place on the basketball court, the Blue cheers whipping at his back. It was Apache time.

In the center of the basketball court, Play Dough shuffled around, nervous and distracted. Beside him, Melman was picking at her cuticles. Jamie and Totle were quizzing each other with random camp trivia that neither knew the answers to.

With the officers in their places and the teams in the bleachers, TJ brought the megaphone to his mouth. "On your marks." Set up in the corner of the court, General Power and General Silver picked up their bows and strung their arrows. "Get set." They pulled back their bowstrings and aimed for the center of their scoring rings. "GO!" The camp roared as the arrows flew.

Play Dough watched it unfold in a flash. The Generals ripped bull's-eyes. Lieutenants Saad and Burrick bounced a tennis ball on their racket in quick buh-bounces. Lieutenants Figg and Kasnett were neck and neck as they swept those same tennis balls through identical obstacle courses of orange cones using brooms. White gained momentum when Lieutenant Kreitzer lapped Lieutenant Finkelstein as they Rollerbladed around the perimeter of the court. White team's General Ferrara swooshed the backward foul shot on her third try, just as General McCarville picked up the basketball to start. On McCarville's sixth try, the basketball hit the backboard and fell through the net! Blue dropped their arms with a collective "Whoosh."

As TJ gave a play-by-play on Lieutenant Wagner's and Lieutenant Shale's chocolate bar ingestion, Play Dough's stomach rumbled. He wasn't hungry, just insanely nervous. He kept seeing flashes of his Gramps beaming as the other Garfinks shared their Color War victory stories over Thanksgiving dinner. He wanted to be showered with congratulatory drumsticks, too, not be the dumb turkey.

"Done!" Wagner cried.

"Open your mouth and stick out your tongue," TJ instructed, checking for any hidden chunks. "And . . . swallowed!"

Play Dough checked out Lieutenant Shale nibbling on a square. He was only halfway through the bar. *C'mon, it's chocolate, not poop!* Shale took another fly-size bite as Wagner passed the baton to Jamie.

"All right, White," the Captain announced. "You'll be quizzed on Rolling Hills history of the 1960s. Blue, when the time comes, you'll be quizzed on Rolling Hills history of the 1980s. A fun reversal. First team to get a question right wins. And I mean WINS." The cheering got eardrum-popping. Play Dough's pits began flooding. Shale needed to hurry the cocoa up. "White," the Captain plowed on. "What were the very first Rolling Hills Color War themes?"

Easy, Play Dough thought. *Blue Hollywood versus White Broadway.* Gramps was General that first summer. For SING, he'd entered the Social Hall in a top hat, cane, and tap shoes, while the Bunker Hillers spritzed him with water à la "Singing in the Rain." Huge success.

Play Dough eyed Totle, who was totally still except for his fingers, which were stroking an invisible beard. Jamie was hopping from foot to foot like she had to pee. Was that a part of her thinking process? "Blue Outerspace versus White Cyberspace!" she cried.

"Incorrect," the Captain said. "The correct answer is Blue Hollywood versus White Broadway. OK, next—"

"I'm done! It's swallowed!" Lieutenant Shale broke in. TJ quickly checked his mouth and nodded with approval. Shale passed the baton to Melman.

“In that case,” the Captain said, “the next question is for Blue.” Play Dough felt a ripple of relief. Then a ripple of nausea. The war really would come down to his wandering smarts. He pressed his temples to keep his brain in place. “In what year of the eighties did the seven-year White streak get broken?” the Captain asked.

Play Dough’s mind raced. He knew it couldn’t be 1984 or 1985, since his Aunt Denise had won in 1984 and his Pops had won in 1985. “1986?” he asked Melman.

“I know nothing,” Melman said. “If you think it’s 1986, go for it.”

“1986!” Play Dough cried.

“Incorrect,” the Captain said. “The correct answer is 1985.”

“Uhhhh.” Play Dough scratched his head. “I think that’s a mistake. 1985 was White Fiction versus Blue Fact. White won.”

“Blue Fact won and that’s a fact,” the Captain said. TJ threw in a cymbal crash: *Ba-dum-tish*.

Play Dough felt his head clog with confusion. He played back all the victory stories his Pops had told him, about how he’d set the record for fastest Rope Burn, and how he’d restrategized Bucket Brigade, and how he’d earned his team one hundred Sportsmanship points with his cheering madness. But *had* his Pops ever said his team had won overall? Now he couldn’t remember.

“Moving on,” the Captain said. “White, what year in the sixties was the Hatchet Hunt tossed over a disqualification?”

Focus, Play Dough told himself, trying to push his blown mind. He watched Jamie and Totle whisper in each other’s ears and then separate with in-sync nods. Totle stepped forward. “1968.”

Play Dough sighed with relief. That couldn't be right. That was the year that Great-Uncle Garfink had found the Hatchet in an apple tree by the Canteen. He'd climbed the tree because his blood sugar was low in the middle of a tennis match and he'd wanted a snack, but then, *voilà!* The Hatchet was just sitting there, nestled in the branches.

Booya! Blue's turn! Play Dough cheered himself on. This was it. This was going to be the question he and Melman guessed correctly. This was going to be the question that turned this war the color of the sea.

"Correct," the Captain said.

Play Dough stumbled forward. *Correct?!* Surely, his ears had missed the "in" part of "incorrect." He waited for the Captain to deliver the right answer. Instead, she tossed the trivia cards in the air. He waited for her to ask Blue a question from memory. Instead, she just stood there, smiling all lovey-dovey at TJ.

Play Dough racked his brain, trying to remember the story just as his Great-Uncle Garfink had told it. Yes, he'd climbed the apple tree. Yes, the Hatchet had just been sitting there. Yes, he'd grabbed it. *Except* . . . Suddenly, Play Dough's memory center lit up like a lightbulb: Great-Uncle Garfink had found the Hatchet *in the middle of a tennis match*! You can't ditch activities to hunt for the Hatchet! Plus, he was buddy-less! The hunt must have been thrown out, just like it had been this summer!

Play Dough took a breath, released some gas, and tried to process it all: He'd thought all his family stories of greatness were about winning. But, now that he looked back on them, no one had actually claimed they'd won—he'd just assumed they had. If the Garfink family was proud of their Color War successes despite losing overall, then did it really matter if he lost overall, too? He'd had so many victories this week—his family's pride couldn't possibly ride on his answers to a few random questions. The Garfinks had left a legacy because they saw themselves as winners, and now, Play Dough thought, maybe so should he.

TJ joined the Captain center court. They kissed, which was . . . weird. "The winner of this summer's Color War," they announced together, "is WHITE!"

White flooded the basketball court with the spirit of a tsunami. Play Dough felt his heart bob around in his chest. He watched Blue clap feebly. He spotted General Power and General McCarville hug sort of lamely. And then Play Dough saw Jenny jumping up and down like a lunatic, holding Jamie's hand, and something inside him burst with happiness.

He threw a Blue Bunker Hiller named Petey, or maybe it was Parker, onto his shoulders and ran up and down the sidelines. "Blue huddle! Blue, don't be blue! You did psychedelic-sauce!" But with the war over and no one leading, the chaos was too chaotic for a mic-less Play Dough to rein in. He put the giggling Bunker Hiller down and felt a tap on his shoulder.

He swung around. It was Jenny. "We've been trying to get your attention," she said with that same beautiful grin.

"Huh?"

She took his sweaty hand and led him to the Faith and Hamburger Hillers, all huddled up. "Now we can group hug for realsies," she said.

Jamie pulled Jenny in and Smelly pulled Play Dough in, and the group squeezed together tightly. Play Dough's nose was buried in Missi's frizz, his arm was tangled with Dover's arm, and his cheek was pressed against Wiener's bony shoulder—it was the best, most awkward, coolest huddle he could ever imagine. "You guys really are the saucest friends ever," he said.

Apparently that pushed a button. The group hug became madder than a madhouse. Everyone started crying and laughing and sputtering nonsense like "Camp can't end! It can't be legal!" and "Camp's the bestest place—I want to take all the hills home with me!" and "I can't, just, I can't!" and "I heart you guys more than life itself!" and "Never let go, Hamburgers, never let go."

Then Jamie started singing the Blue alma mater: *"So hug it out and let me in, hey friend, we win . . ."* Then Jenny started singing the White alma mater: *"Each day goes quickly, cherish the moments, don't let them pass . . ."* Soon enough everyone was singing their opponent's almas with and over one another. Once Play Dough and Smelly launched into their falsettos, though, the group cracked up and let the almas go. Everyone de-clumped a little, and their huddle became a circle.

"You see?" Jenny said. "No matter what, we're always friends at the end of the war."

Jamie giggled, wiping her tearstained cheeks. "But there were a lot of hoops this time around."

"I guess," Jenny said. She looked at Play Dough and he swore her eyes sparkled. "But it was worth jumping through every last one."

Brian, my favorite grandson,

(Anyone asks, I have no favorites.)

As you probably know, I got in a very big fight with a golf cart. But if you think I look bad, you should see the cart! Just kidding—the cart's fine. Golf goes on.

In response to your letter: Congratulations on Lieutenant! I will potato fist bump you in person when I see you after camp. It might be too late, but nevertheless, here's my advice: 1) Lead with Garfink humor—fart jokes never get old. 2) Make strong friendships in the trenches. And 3) cherish every second of the war.

From one Officer Garfink to another, enclosed in this package is my Color War shirt from Rolling Hills' opening summer. Tear the plastic and wear it proud. You and me, kid. We're the craziest legends out there.

I'm so proud of you and the man you've become.

Givin' you all my lovin',

Gramps

Burying the Hatchet

"Here it is!" Play Dough said, grandly gesturing to a sorry, hacked-up tree stump in the middle of the forest.

Jenny tried to smile, but it turned into a yawn. She'd dance-partied it up with the Faith Hillers until five in the morning, and so had almost bailed on Play Dough's plan to meet before reveille. But now she was glad she'd dragged herself out of bed. She'd always dreamed of standing where the Color War officers held their traditional end-of-war ceremony. She was told from past Lieutenants that they typically stood in a circle around the tree stump, alternating White and Blue, rooting on the Hatchet finder as he or she hacked it with the Color War Hatchet. Their version of "burying the hatchet," or making peace.

She guessed the ceremony would happen today, just that no one would hack, or the Generals would, or something. Thinking about her missed opportunity made her skin prickle with regret. "If only I hadn't blown it," she said, "we'd be a part of the ceremony in a few hours, and we wouldn't have to sneak here all alone."

Play Dough shrugged. "Actually, I'm glad it worked out this way. It's cool being here, just you and me."

And just like that, the regret melted. "I guess you're right." She stepped on the stump and admired the rising sun breaking through the branches. Some of the light bounced off of Play Dough's helmet of gelled hair. He looked really handsome, considering it was the crack of dawn. It was kind of a reversal, actually, since she was the one who hadn't showered since yesterday, was still wearing her SING costume, and had bags under her eyes. "So how are we supposed to do this without a Hatchet?" she asked. "Mime it?"

"Miming could work," Play Dough began, reaching into his backpack, "but real hacking would be way better." He whipped out Eddie's Hatchet.

Jenny screamed with joy. It rang through the morning fog. "Did you steal it back?!" she asked.

"Nah, Eddie let me borrow it." He laughed. "But I did steal this from the Shirt Donation Box in the tie-dye nook." He pulled from his backpack an extra-large blue T-shirt. "I made this part," he said, showing her the back where it read HATCHET HERO in a combo of iron-on letters and faded Sharpie marker.

Normally, Jenny's first instinct would be to list everything gross about it: the size, the stains, the fact that it looked like a drunk kindergartner had decorated it with a blindfold on. But not today. The new Jenny saw fashion-forward. And passion. And versatility. Since Jamie and Missi could fit inside it with her, it would make amazing friendship apparel. "I LOVE IT!"

she cried, pulling it over her head. It fell to her knees, like a moomoo. She twirled, feeling the forest shadows and glowing sun hit her like a strobe light.

Jenny plopped dizzily to the stump, sighing with delight, and Play Dough joined her. Their knees knocked. After a few seconds of comfortable silence, Play Dough broke in: "So, I found out what the Hatchet Hunt clues meant."

"Omigod, I forgot about them!" Jenny gasped. "Wait, what were they again?"

"*Lady and the Tramp* was the first clue."

Lady and the . . . "Lady and the Tramp*oline*!" Jenny exclaimed.

"Bingo! And 'Dryer Sheets'—think about brand names."

Jenny forced her sleep-deprived brain to cooperate. *Downy, no, um, um, oh!* "Bounce!"

"Yup!" Play Dough said. "And the third clue—'Toil and Trouble'—this one's kind of a stretch. Toil rhymes with—"

"Coil!" Jenny cried. "The Hatchet was buried in the coil of the trambopoline!"

"Wow. Yeah. You're, uhhhh . . ."

Smart, pretty, fun? Jenny caught Play Dough staring into her eyes like they were magnets. It made her belly rebirth all those butterflies she'd felt a few days ago. Then, randomly, his fingers were hovering over her head.

"Can I touch your hair?" he asked.

She smiled, remembering how he'd touched her hair the night before Color War broke. What was once so weird now seemed sweet. "This part," she said, offering him a chunk of the bottom.

He ran his fingers through it. "C'mon, you must put Bounce in your hair—it's so soft."

"Moroccan Oil, actually." She grinned. "You know what else is soft?" she asked, touching her finger to her lips.

Play Dough felt her lips. "Not as soft as your hair, but—"

Jenny laughed. "That's not what I meant!"

He put his finger on her nose. "Is that what you meant?" Then between her eyes. "What about this?" Then on her ear. "Oh yeah, the lobe's real soft."

Jenny was giggling so hard she couldn't breathe. "Omigod, no, that was your cue to—!" And then, just as she was about to say, "Kiss me," he kissed her.

Oh, the butterflies. They were fluttering up a summer storm. After three Mississippi she pulled away. Her heart was so full, she was afraid it might burst. "Ready to hack?" she asked, holding out the Hatchet.

He held the handle, his fingers stacked on top of hers. "Ready."

1ST

GROOVY
COLOR WAR

Acknowledgments

A few years ago, I was lucky to collaborate with the Spiegel brothers—Adam and David—on writing the musical *Camp Rolling Hills*. My friend Erica Finkel saw a workshop of the show and tossed out the idea that I write a book for middle schoolers. A few months later, I embarked on *Camp Rolling Hills*: the Book! Erica is my fairy godmother, bestie, and editor, who grew the seed of an idea into a full-fledged series. I am forever grateful. Thank you to the amazing Spiegel brothers for your inspiration and permission to nurture the world we hold so close to our hearts.

Camp has been a major part of my life and still is. I was lucky to transition from camper to counselor to upper staff at Tyler Hill Camp, where my mom was the Head of Girls' Side. Mom and Dad, thank you for introducing me to this incredible, life-changing place, for daring me to be silly and take enormous risks, and for your endless love and support. To my brother, Mike, my sister, Amy, and my sister-in-law, Deanna, who all work in the camp industry: Congrats on making a career out of the greatest cult. I love you.

Grandma Terry, Grandma Joanie, and Grandpa Lenny—

thank you for being my number one fans. You three are the world's best.

Lauren Kasnett Nearpass, thank you for brainstorming marketing and branding and for inviting me to blog for Summer 365. I'm honored to be working with you and your incredible organization.

Aimee Berger, you're a rock star. Thank you for all your summer camp coordination and support! Tyler Hill Camp and Camp Louise: Facilitating workshops with your campers was truly magical.

Jay Jacobs, thank you for conceiving the STARFISH Program and for granting me permission to reference it in the Camp Rolling Hills series. It's a brilliant values system that defined so much of my personal experience at Tyler Hill. I'm so glad I can share it. Lexi Korologos, my teenage life coach, thank you for reading drafts, dishing your honest feedback, and brainstorming titles.

To my brave students at Long Island City High School and Naked Angels, thank you for inspiring me every single day with your lack of inhibition. You keep my imagination fed.

To my Bunk 4 Cauliflowers, thanks for finding the "True Colors" alma mater I wrote for your freshmen SING in 2002. You'll always be my little onions.

Thank you to my friend and collaborator Elissa Brent Weissman for the blurb, the collaborative camp-themed book events, and for always reading what I send you.

Thank you to Erica Rand Silverman and Nell Pierce at Sterling Lord Literistic, and my theatrical literary agent at

Creative Artists Agency, Ally Shuster, who's always such a fierce advocate of my work.

Susan Van Metre, Erica Finkel (again and again), and the whole brilliant team at Abrams: Pam, Jim, Samantha, Mary, Elisa, Rebecca, and Kyle, thank you for seeing so much potential in an early draft and for providing the feedback that has enriched the story a million times over. A special shout-out to Caitlin Miller for kicking butt and dealing so gracefully with my million emails a week. And illustrator Melissa Manwill, so happy to be collaborating with you and your character sketches. They're perfection.

My camp friends. My campers. My counselors. My co-counselors. The camps: Twin Oaks, Crestwood, Summit, Tyler Hill, A.C.T., Oxbridge. You have made me who I am today and provided me with the heart and experience to write this series.

My partner-in-crime, Tim Borecky, thank you for lending me your wisdom and dramaturgy every time I cornered you to read you chapters. I appreciate your indulging my characters as if they are our friends.

To all the camp people out there, enjoy the adventure and the s'mores. And remember, the only war worth fighting is Color War.